EXTRAORDINARY WORLD

MARY FRAME

This book is dedicated to you, dear reader.
Thank you for continuing this story, despite that terrible
cliffhanger in the last one.
I know, I hate me, too.
But I still love you all <3

CHAPTER ONE

"Paige?" I'm frozen in the doorway to Jared's house.

She's here. But she's not supposed to be here, she's supposed to be at the rendezvous point. My brain stutters to a stop, failing to work through the implications, but my wicked, traitorous eyes keep going, taking in every detail and presenting the scene to me with malicious glee.

Illuminated by the porch lights, she's standing at the bottom of the short flight of steps that leads to the gravel drive. She's still in the new dress she wore to the dance. Her eyes are red and mascara streaks down her face like charcoal tears.

And she's not alone.

"You can have her back as soon as you fix our little problem." Red-tipped nails grip Paige's shoulder like talons. It's a voice I recognize. A voice I've gone to great pains to never hear again.

Shock pulses through me.

They're here.

At Jared's.

He's sleeping peacefully less than a hundred feet away.

And the parents, the people I've been running from for months, have found me. And they have Paige.

"You see," Mother says, "you stole a bit of money from us, and now you're going to pay it back. With interest."

That's why they're here? Money? What we took was a mere trifle to them, a two-bit con.

My brain struggles to process the scene in front of me.

Mother looks the same as always: hair pulled back into a neat chignon, white blouse and dark pencil skirt perfectly pressed, face smoothed with Botox, and a slight smile that masquerades as friendly and unassuming and in reality is anything but. She could be a secretary for the CEO of a million-dollar company, or a wealthy heiress dressed to volunteer at a benefit gala.

But appearances are deceiving. She's none of those things. And she's standing in front of me with everything I hold dear in the palms of her hands.

I have to get Paige away from her. Nothing else matters.

I glance behind Mother and into the darkness. Where's Father?

There's a car parked behind the station wagon, a new-model black Mercedes, its interior dark as midnight. It's running with its lights on, and I have to assume Father is watching everything unfold.

What do I do? Maybe if I just agree . . . I shut the front door to Jared's house behind me so our voices won't filter inside and wake him up. I step closer, stopping at the top of the stairs. "Fine. I'll pay you back. We took, what, three thousand dollars? I'll give you six grand if you give me Paige and leave us alone."

She laughs.

It's not a happy laugh. It's more of a Cruella De Vil, "I want to kill your puppies" kind of cackle.

I grit my teeth.

"That's not what I'm talking about, but then you have always been on the slow side. You were supposed to seduce Wallace, and you left before we could finish the con. I think he was worth quite a bit more than what you took from us."

The voice I remember so well, laced with condescension, makes my jaw clench.

I had almost forgotten how much I hate it. It's worse than nails on a chalkboard. It's more like metal on a cheese grater.

"What do you want me to do?"

"It's quite simple. We don't have time for a long con, but since you're so cozy with the locals, you can help us. All you have to do is introduce us to the new friends you've made here. Tell them we're your aunt and uncle, the only family you have left. If you trust us, so will they. You can start with your little boyfriend here." Her eyes flick behind me, taking in the large house.

A con in Castle Cove? On Jared?

My heart thumps a death knell in my chest. I mean, really, it's what I've been doing already but . . . what exactly are they planning?

It doesn't matter. I have to get Paige away from her. For that, I'll promise anything and deal with the consequences later.

My eyes flick from Paige's tear-streaked face to Mother's narrowed eyes.

"You have a problem with that?"

"Not if you let go of Paige. And she gets to stay with me while we run the con."

I know I've overstepped when she laughs again, the sound louder and even more grating than before. "Why, exactly, would we do that? If you have Paige, what's to keep you from running away again? We need collateral."

And now I argue for my life. "If you take Paige now, I have no reason to help you. I won't work with you or do anything you say unless she's with me. And as you've said, you'll need me if you're going to con this town."

She pauses, which I hope is a good sign. "That's how you'll treat us, after we've been helping you this whole time?"

"What do you mean, helping me this whole time?" Even as the words leave my mouth, my stomach sinks with suspicion.

"Who do you think got you your most recent job with the PD? If it weren't for us staging a little B and E at your place, you wouldn't have gotten so close to your little boyfriend." She smirks. "Something you seem to be taking full advantage of."

"So it was you who broke into Ruby's." I make it a statement, knowing she won't answer a question. The rose was too much of a coincidence, so I already knew they were involved somehow. Plus, Ruby's was the only place that didn't fit. It wasn't in line with the senior center and the bluffs, and Miss Viola didn't have keys for it. Thankfully, no one else has pieced that together. But why would the parents do it in the first place? And how did they know to stage it to match the other incidents around town?

She shrugs. "Of course it was us. It wasn't hard to figure out what was happening around town and take advantage of it, even without the police scanner. People around here are only too eager to gossip."

"So you did it to get me involved with the cops?"

"We're going to need your connections in the community if this con is going to work."

"No. It's only going to work if you leave Paige with me." My eyes keep drawing back to Paige. She's not speaking, barely moving, her eyes focused on the ground. My stomach lurches. I have to get her away from them.

"And why would we do that?"

"If you really want my help, you'll have to. I won't do it any other way."

"You know, there isn't a court in this land that would take her from us if we claim her."

Exactly what I've been thinking. I can't let it come to that. "If you take Paige, then I won't run your con. What exactly is the scam you want to do?"

"For now, your job is to tell your little boyfriend here that your aunt and uncle, David and Leah Hampton, are in town for a bit."

The same names they used at the hotel.

"We're here to visit with our nieces. And if anyone asks, we're retired but we volunteer and do a lot of charity work."

Charity. Really?

"Now. If you want to take Paige, we're going to need some other kind of collateral to make sure you don't run."

If you want to take Paige. So maybe she's realized we're at an impasse and something's got to give to get us what we both want. "What kind of collateral?"

She jerks her head to my newly purchased station wagon. "Both of you get in the back seat."

"You didn't answer my question. Where are you planning on taking us?" I try to keep the edge of panic out of my voice but fail.

"Stop being so dramatic. We're taking you to that hovel of a shop you're calling home."

"How do I know that's the truth?"

"Would you rather wake your little boyfriend in there instead? We could introduce ourselves now."

What do I do? Wake Jared and deal with the fallout, not knowing what they'll do or say to explain their presence here, or go with them?

Where else would they take us? What would they do with us?

"If you want us to trust you not to run off with your sister, you have to trust me right now. Otherwise, we'll leave you here and she's coming with us. And neither of you will make a noise about it because you don't want anyone waking up now, do you?"

I swallow. She's right. I don't have a choice. Will they really leave Paige with me? Even just for now? Until I can figure something else out . . .

My eyes go back to Paige, who's still standing there with Mother's hand on her tense shoulder, her gaze focused downward.

"Fine."

Mother hesitates for a few seconds. Her eyes bore into mine, trying to read me. "Here." She releases her grip on Paige's shoulder. "As a show of good faith."

Paige stands stock still for a few long seconds, her eyes wide like a trapped bird who can't quite believe it's been sprung.

I can't believe it either. Mother let her go. Why? There's always a reason. She intended to release Paige to me this whole time, I'm sure. What is their real plan?

We meet in the middle of the porch steps and she throws her arms around my waist.

"Now that I've shown I'm willing to compromise, it's your turn. Get in the car." Mother opens the back seat door and waits.

With my arms around a trembling Paige, I consider my options. Go inside? What if they come to the door and expose me? The only other option is leaving with them. What if they have something else up their sleeve and it's not going back to Ruby's?

I swallow past a lump in my throat, panic threatening to spill out and overwhelm me entirely.

I have to stay calm and think. Panic won't help Paige.

If they truly want to use my connections here to run a con, it wouldn't be in their best interest to do anything harmful. Besides, if they just wanted Paige, they could have taken her by now and run without coming to find me at all. They must really want this con; otherwise, why show up here, now, dangling her in front of me?

With my arms still around Paige's slight form, we walk together to the car.

Mother slides into the driver's seat and I get in the back with Paige.

Our getaway bag is on the floor and I grab it and hold it tightly in my lap. All of the money I've been saving is inside. If we ever have any hope of leaving Castle Cove and the parents behind, we'll need it.

"Keys." Mother holds her hand up in the air.

I pull Ruby's house key off the loop and drop the car keys into her hand.

The engine turns over with a shudder and a groan and she makes a derisive noise. "This car is a hunk of junk. You couldn't do better?"

Not without breaking a law or two, but I hold my tongue.

The ride is quiet and tense. Paige is stiff as a rock, leaning against me in the back seat of the car. I focus on my breathing, in and out, in and out.

We're both in shock, I think. The Mercedes follows us the entire way.

We pull up in front of Ruby's, and Paige and I scramble out of the back seat like the devil is on our heels.

I hand Paige the house key and murmur for her to get inside.

She doesn't even question me, just takes the key and runs to the front door. I stay on the walkway, halfway between the car and the house.

Mother is still in the running station wagon.

Father climbs out of the Mercedes. He looks the same as always, dressed in expensive but comfortable slacks and a button-up shirt that fits like it was made for his lithe frame. He stops next to Mother's open window and leans in to tell her something I can't hear.

Then he turns toward me. "We're taking your car so you won't be tempted to leave." He moves in my direction, stopping a few feet away. "Where are you keeping the money you were planning on using for your little getaway?"

"I don't have any money."

He laughs, the sound dark and unbelieving. "We all know that's a lie. Hand it over or I'll go inside and get Paige right now, and you won't be able to stop me." His eyes are hard.

He could overpower me, break into the house. They've gotten into Ruby's before, after all. Is there no safe place?

Swallowing, I reach into my bag and pull out the wrapped wad of bills, placing it quickly in his open palm to avoid any physical contact.

"Good girl. We'll be in touch."

He gets back into the Mercedes and then they both drive away, Mother taking our newly acquired station wagon with her.

Still reeling from the entire experience, I head into the house, locking the door behind me like it will protect us from anything.

Paige is sitting on the couch in the living room. I go to the kitchen and make tea, needing to do something with my trembling hands and buzzing thoughts. It doesn't take long. When the tea is done, I find Paige sitting on the couch in the living room and sit next to her, handing her a mug.

"This is all my fault." Her voice is full of tears.

"What happened?"

"They found me when I left school." The words waver slightly as they leave her mouth.

We had planned on meeting on a quiet street between the school and Ruby's an hour into the dance. The parents, having bugged our phones and listened in on our last conversation about Paige staying until the very end, were supposed to have taken the bait and gotten occupied by the crowd of people picking up their kids at the school. Paige was supposed to have been long gone by then. Nothing is going as it was supposed to.

"Did they hurt you?"

"No. They told me if I came with them and did what they said, they wouldn't turn you in. Then they were completely silent the rest of the ride here." She shivers. "It was so creepy. What are we going to do?" Her small frame, already huddled on the couch next to me, droops even further. I rub her shoulder.

I don't have an answer yet. "It'll be okay."

How can it ever be okay? I don't know. The words are meaningless, but I can't stand to see Paige hurting. It makes me want to punch things. Or cry. Or throw myself onto the floor and have a tantrum, wailing about the injustice of it all. But I can't do any of those things. If we're going to find our way out of this, I have to stay strong and sharp.

I have to protect Paige.

"This is all my fault," she says.

"It's not your fault, Paige. They would have found us no matter what."

They would have. They were onto us the entire time.

But how?

How did they find us?

I thought I was so careful . . . but they've always been two steps ahead of me.

My jaw clenches.

I *hate* them.

"We would have had to deal with them eventually. They would have found us, even if we had managed to leave Castle Cove. They'll never give up. Maybe it's better to get it over with now. Confront them and get them off our backs for good."

"Really? How is it better? You know what they're going to want you to do." Her hair—which had been fashioned into an intricate bun for the dance—is now in disarray, strands flying around her shoulders like wisps of frayed ribbons.

I do. Mother said as much. A con here. In Castle Cove.

My stomach clenches and my heart hurts.

We sit on the couch, staring in silence at the blank TV.

"I'll think of something, Paige. I will. I promise. We'll get out of this." I mean the words, but even as I say them, I have no idea how to pull one over on them. I never have.

"How?"

"I . . . don't know. Yet. But I will. I'll think of something." I inject as much confidence into my voice as I can. I *have* to think of something. "In the meantime, there's not much we can do except wait and see. Why don't you go get some sleep?"

She nods uncertainly, her eyes red and bleary. Her steps are slow as she makes her way upstairs, her bag still on her back.

Once her door shuts softly, I close my eyes and slump back on the couch.

My worst nightmare has come true.

CHAPTER TWO

The sound of muffled voices pulls me from sleep.

Bleary-eyed, I blink my eyes open. I'm on the couch. There's a blanket over me. It's from my bed. It wasn't there when I fell asleep. I sit up. And wince. There's a crick in my neck, and the smell of flour and syrup wafts through the air.

Is Paige cooking? Curious to see such an oddity in action, I turn my head toward the sounds, moving carefully when my neck twinges.

I can't see who's in the kitchen, but I can hear Paige's voice. She's not alone, and she's definitely not cooking. It's Jared.

He asks Paige if she wants to go to the beach, maybe eat lunch on the boardwalk to celebrate the end of the school year, chatting as if our entire world hasn't just imploded.

Paige's affirmative response sounds normal, if a bit subdued.

The previous night comes rushing back, raging in my mind, filtering down into my stomach. I'm going to get an ulcer. What I really want to do is curl up in a ball and forget the world. But I can't. I'm not ready to face Jared, though. Not yet.

Why is he here anyway? I stand up and nearly step on Gravy. The cat hisses at me and takes off, claws scraping against the floor as he flees down the hall into the front of the shop.

Jared must have come over to bring the devil cat home.

I pause, listening. They're still talking in the kitchen, so they must not have heard Gravy. The cat apparently hates me again.

Keeping my footsteps light, I sneak upstairs to the bathroom to freshen up.

The woman in the mirror looks like she's been through a tornado. My eyes are puffy, my hair is tangled, and the mascara smudges under my eyes make me look a level below zombie and maybe half a step above corpse.

I clean up and brush my hair, my brain shuffling the entire time. With all of the craziness of last night, I haven't had a chance to think about Jared and what happened with him before the world exploded in my face.

What am I going to do?

We slept together. But it was more than that. We had . . . everything between us, for a few glorious moments. I opened up because I never thought I would see him again, and now he's downstairs with Paige like nothing has changed.

But it has.

I imagine, for a minute, pushing him away. Again. Making some excuse about why we can't be together.

It's what I should do.

It's what's best for him.

But I can't.

Mother's words haunt me. *You can start with your little boyfriend here.*

The entire time I've known him, he's thought of me as Ruby. That alone is bad enough to twist my insides and make me groan in frustration every time he calls me by *her* name. But it's also something that I could possibly, maybe, if I got caught and had to do it, rationalize and defend. But now . . . now I have no idea what's going to happen with the parents, but I doubt it will be something I can easily explain. The vines of my lies will grow into a forest of deception, and all for what?

For Paige.

They want me to introduce them to everyone as my aunt and uncle, allude to their charity business, but what else? How much will they demand?

I don't want to do what they say or go along with their scheme, but there's a small part of me that revels in the ruse. With Jared, it won't be a deception at all to continue our relationship. My time with him is limited. If I do as they say, I get to keep him, if only for a little while longer. I'll have pretend feelings for him that aren't pretend at all.

My palms sweat when I think about seeing him again. About being with him again.

For now, I have to act like everything is normal. What else can I do? I need to come up with a plan. How am I going to get us out of this mess? I'm back to having no car, no money, and no means of escape.

Back downstairs in the kitchen, Jared is flipping pancakes at the stove and Paige is leaning against the counter.

She looks okay, although there's a wilt in the line of her shoulders. At least Jared has put a bit of sparkle back in her eyes.

She's so resilient.

"Do you want to go to the beach today?" she asks when I enter the kitchen.

My eyes are on Jared, eating him up. Apparently he can put the sparkle back in me, as well.

Despite everything else.

Last night, I never thought I would see him again. But here we are. I don't know whether to laugh or cry.

He's in a pair of swim trunks with a plain T-shirt and sandals on his feet. The clock on the oven shows nine o'clock. He missed his morning run to come by.

I'm totally checking him out and he knows it—and likes it—if the smirk on his face is any indication.

"Ruby?" Paige interrupts my not-so-subtle perusal.

"What?"

"Did you hear me?"

"Um. Yeah, sure. Beach good."

I've devolved into a caveman. The things this man does to my brain.

"Good morning," Jared says. He's not fooled at all by my lack of speaking ability. "Do you want coffee?"

He made me coffee. My already melting heart melts a little more. "Yes."

The coffee pot is right next to the stove. He opens the cabinet and gets me a mug, placing it on the counter.

When I step up beside him to get my cup, he stares down at me, his eyes heavy with the weight of the night before.

"Naomi is leaving for camp today, so I'm glad we're doing something," Paige says from seemingly far away. "It's going to suck to be here without her all summer." That's not the only reason this summer is going to suck, but we can't talk about that now.

Normalcy.

We can do it.

Jared rips his eyes away from mine to glance over at Paige. He clears his throat and turns back to the stove. "That's too bad. Where's she going to camp?"

I pour my coffee in silence as they talk about some summer camp up in the middle of the forest next to a lake, a few hours away.

What would he have done just now if Paige weren't here?

"Are you ready for pancakes, Paige?" Jared expertly flips one onto a plate.

"Yes." She walks up on the other side with her plate and then grabs the syrup off the counter. "I'm eating in the living room." With an eye roll worthy of her age, she bolts into the other room.

"Are you hungry?" he asks once she's gone.

"Yes." But not for pancakes.

We turn toward each other at the same time and then his mouth is on mine, the heat burning between us.

He bites my lower lip as he pulls away, his arms still around me. "Why did you leave me the note?"

Shit.

Oh, yeah. I left a note.

"I . . . had to leave to pick up Paige from the dance."

"Why would you apologize for that?"

Thankfully, it was a vague note. Two words, *I'm sorry*. Sorry for lying, sorry for leaving, sorry for getting him involved at all. He would have understood if Paige and I had disappeared like we had planned.

All of the emotions of last night come rushing back, the pain of having to leave him, knowing we only had one night together, mixed with the pleasure of being with him and the anxiety from the parents' sudden arrival. What a mess.

At least it's an easy thing to explain.

"I felt bad that I had to leave you." And it's not even a lie.

He smiles, a small tilt of his lips that I could stare at forever. "We could have a redo. Tonight."

We could. I mean, we really could. "Okay, but what about Paige?"

He shrugs and rubs my shoulders. "You could just tell her about us."

"Too late," Paige says from the doorway.

I jump away from Jared, like we're guilty teenagers caught necking in the family room, but he manages to snag my hand and hang on.

She frowns, her face stern. But then she breaks into a smile. "Seriously, like I didn't see this coming? Adults are weird. Can I have more pancakes?"

Jared turns to the stove, pouring more batter into the pan. "Of course."

While his back is turned, Paige gives me a side-eye with raised brows. I know she's asking, *Are you sure about this?*

I shrug.

It might be the only thing in my life, besides Paige, that will get me through this crisis. Or it could make everything epically worse.

~*~

The beach is bright and happy enough to almost make me forget about our troubles.

Just kidding. I could never forget the looming threat of the parents, no matter how hard I try to act normal. Even if by some miracle they don't take Paige and we get away, they've proven that they'll follow us anyway. The last time we escaped, we had the element of surprise, a plan, and cash. This time, we have none of those things, and *they* have some ridiculous scheme that will get me arrested. Then who will take care of Paige? Jared flashes me a warm smile, but it leaves me ice-cold.

What if *Jared* has to arrest me?

We splash in the surf and eat lunch in the sand before heading back home. On the outside, we're picture-perfect, except for my tendency to scan the area every so often. I can't help it. Everywhere we go, I'm on the lookout. As a result, the few times Jared leans in for a kiss, I turn my head. And I don't let him hold my hand for more than a few seconds.

It's probably ridiculous. It's not like I can protect him completely from their machinations, or mine. They already know about us, obviously.

Ugh.

I don't want them to see how much he affects me. It's not safe for him. How can I protect him and still act normal around him? I can't.

And it bothers him.

His lips turn down every time I shy away, and the crease between his brows gets deeper as the afternoon progresses.

At the end of the day it doesn't matter, because I don't see the parents. Then there is a moment, a brief span where I think someone is tailing us when we're heading back to Ruby's, but when Jared turns down our street, they pass us by. It's not a black Mercedes or the old clunky station wagon. It's just a nondescript sedan like nearly every other car in Castle Cove.

For dinner, Jared makes us spaghetti and we watch *Gone with the Wind* in the living room.

Paige lounges on the floor on a couple of pillows while I sit with Jared on the couch, more comfortable leaning against him now since we're not in public and the threat of malicious, watching eyes aren't a potential problem.

It's almost normal.

Jared doesn't seem to feel the tension simmering in the air, an ever-present and lingering anxiety I can't seem to shake.

If I didn't know Paige better, I wouldn't be able to tell, but every now and then, I catch the slight crease in her cheek, the turn of her lip.

She's worried.

So am I.

Paige falls asleep before we even reach intermission, exhausted from lack of sleep the night before and then the day spent in the sun.

Jared's arm is around me, comforting and warm, and I could fall asleep, too, if it weren't for the brush of his thumb on my shoulder sending zings of electricity straight to my core every time he moves.

In silent accord—after Scarlett declares she'll never be hungry again and the sweeping music signals the midpoint of the movie—I shut off the TV.

Jared carries Paige up to her room, having trouble coordinating her gangly limbs up the stairs, knocking her into the staircase once. She sleeps through it, but we giggle like teenagers.

After making sure all the doors are locked and the lights are off, I follow him up the stairs.

Leaning in the doorway, the light shining in from the hallway behind me, I watch him tuck Paige in, pulling her covers over her sleeping form and silently turning off her lamp.

He moves in my direction, and I take his hand, shutting Paige's door gently before dragging him over to the master bedroom.

This man.

I wait until the door to the bedroom has shut before I grab his head and pull it down, the weight of the day still heavy in my heart but lightened by his hands down my back. He pulls me against him.

"Jared," I breathe, wanting to tell him everything I feel, everything I need, but unable to form the words.

So instead, I show him.

My hands paint my emotions across his skin, every caress, every glance, every movement, until we fall asleep in each other's arms.

The morning starts with pure bliss.

I've never woken up with someone. Never experienced tangled limbs, quiet laughs, and secret smiles.

I've never felt so comfortable in my own skin, with heated eyes and lingering glances that tell me more than words could how beautiful I am.

I've never made waffles and laughed so hard my sides hurt. I've never had someone's hands finding excuses to touch, excuses for mouths to taste.

It's amazing.

And temporary.

Paige leaves our annoying couple-ness for the sanctity of her bedroom.

It's Sunday, but Jared has to go to work, and I have to open the shop since we closed yesterday to go play at the beach. There are already a few customers waiting outside. After we eat I walk him to the door.

"I'll call you." He presses a kiss, quick and soft, to my mouth before I open the door.

He nods at some of the waiting customers. There are only a few.

Mrs. Hale is first in line, ready for her weekly chat, and there's another couple behind her. At a glance, they appear to be tourists.

I'm so focused on Jared while he greets Mrs. Hale and then moves past her that I don't focus on any of the other customers waiting.

It's not until they stop Jared, and I've said hello to Mrs. Hale, that I realize they aren't random tourists.

I see the curve of the woman's cheek and the slope of the man's nose every time I look in the mirror.

The euphoria of the morning evaporates in a single glance.

It's them. And they're talking to Jared.

CHAPTER THREE

The parents always time their tactics with surgical precision.

Mrs. Hale pulls me inside but not before I catch a snippet of their conversation.

"You must be Jared." Mother stops him with a gentle hand on his arm, the smile on her face lighting up her eyes. "I'm Ruby's aunt Leah, and this is my husband, David."

Jared's brows lift and then Mrs. Hale is taking my arm and handing me a tray of cookies, forcing me to look away. They're pudding cookies, she tells me—but she calls them "puddin' cookies."

I play it cool, like everything is perfectly normal, while talking to Mrs. Hale and simultaneously eavesdropping on the conversational disaster happening just outside the open door.

In my imagination they're telling him the truth—well, their version of the truth—about all of my lies and deceptions, begging him to help them get back their daughter while Jared gapes at me in horror. But that's just my imagination. In reality, the words are normal chitchat and introductions.

Mrs. Hale tells me she's baking again. A fleeting glimmer of pride flickers through me despite my inattention and anxiety. I know she hasn't baked since her husband died because of the guilt she felt. She's finally moving on, and I wonder if I had something to do with her progress. The feeling is short-lived.

"Ruby, darling, you didn't tell us you had so many wonderful friends." Mother steps up next to me, putting an arm around my shoulders and squeezing me lightly, the sincerest smile covering her face.

She introduces herself to Mrs. Hale and I meet Jared's eyes.

He has a question in his gaze, probably wondering why I didn't mention my relatives were in town, or why I haven't mentioned them at all, ever.

I try to view them through his eyes, what details he must be taking in.

They've dressed the part of rich, middle-aged tourists. Mother's linen pants are professionally pressed and spotless, her shoulder-length dark hair flowing softly around her face. Father's polo shirt is appropriately expensive—as are the brand-name sunglasses perched on his head, covering some of his salt-and-pepper hair.

If I didn't know them so well, I might think they were an attractive couple.

"I have to get to work," Jared finally says, releasing me from the misery of being in the same room with him and *them.* "It was nice to meet you both." He gives me a small smile and a nod but doesn't have a chance to say anything further because Father speaks.

"We have to get together soon for dinner or drinks. Do you play golf?" He claps a hand on Jared's upper back, like they're already friends or something, and walks with him to the door.

Meanwhile, Mother is schmoozing with Mrs. Hale. She's already helped herself to a cookie, and she's savoring it and gushing about how amazing it is and how Mrs. Hale simply must share the recipe.

Poor Mrs. Hale, she hardly knows what's hit her. She takes the compliments with a bright smile and flushing face. She's already so much under Mother's spell she thinks it's her own idea to leave the shop and let the family do their catching up, and then she's out the door, still smiling while she walks away.

Once Jared and Mrs. Hale are gone, I turn to the elephants in the room. Except they're less like elephants and more like hyenas, eating their young and killing for sport.

"What do you want?" I ask from behind the cash register, putting the counter between us like it'll protect me.

"Is that any way to greet your dearest parents?" Father asks, his expression wounded.

"The place is . . . *cozy.*" Mother flicks an invisible piece of dust from her arm. "You couldn't have done better?" One perfectly plucked brow lifts in my direction.

I remain silent. They wouldn't understand.

Father sidles over to my side, leaning over the counter and getting a look at the cash register. "As far as cons go, this psychic farce isn't the best deal." He frowns at the antique-looking setup and then turns his head to face me. "Although hooking up with the cop will be good for us. We'll have an in on the local crime scene."

"Is he doing any business on the side?" She's asking if he's using his position of authority to make extra money. Illegally.

I don't answer.

"You didn't tell your little boyfriend about us." Father pulls a small metal case out of his pocket and flicks it open, pulling out a toothpick.

"I haven't had time."

He sticks the toothpick in the corner of his mouth. A habit he's had for as long as I can remember. If he's not smoking, he has one of those damn mint toothpicks in his mouth. "Really? Even though you spent all yesterday together? It was what you promised to do, when we let you take Paige, you remember."

"I remember."

"It doesn't matter. We'll tell you now."

Mother cuts in. "Since you spent all day yesterday prancing around the beach with the cop, we've been doing a bit of work around town.

There're so many options here. Really, this town is perfect. Ninety percent of the population is retired."

"Like your neighbor." Father nods in the direction of Mr. Bingel's, but his eyes stay focused on me, gauging my reaction.

"He doesn't have any money," I say.

"Sure he does. Not like our normal marks, maybe, but he's got enough. He's a retired widower. No living children. And his son was in the military. They pay pretty well when someone dies on active duty. I bet that house is completely paid off. He's got something stashed away."

I struggle to maintain a blank expression, not wanting them to see how their words affect me. Mr. Bingel isn't some haughty millionaire or faceless mark. He's my friend. "He just adopted a couple of kids. I bet there's not much money left."

It's a weak argument, and I know I've made a mistake as soon as the words leave my mouth. He's circling the pack and hunting for the lame, the isolated, the weak. And by trying to protect Mr. Bingel, I've just put my head between his bone-crushing teeth.

Father's face is hard, his eyes sharp and assessing. "You don't get to debate this. We're going to tell you what you're going to do, and you're going to do it. Or we expose you and take Paige. Even if you don't serve jail time, you definitely won't see Paige ever again. Courts favor parents in these circumstances, and even though we tried so hard to help you . . ." He tsks and shakes his head.

"You just won't change. Lying, stealing, and kidnapping your sister. They won't let you live within a mile of a school once we're done with you."

"Crossing state lines with a minor you don't have custody of is a federal charge," Mother puts in, her face smug. "And that's all before they realize you're not Ruby. You've been defrauding the cops. No one will believe you're not the bad guy."

My stomach drops with their words. There has to be some way out of this.

"Are you going to tell me what you want me to do then? The neighbor isn't going to be enough for you, I'm sure." I take a slow breath, bracing myself for their verdict.

They exchange another glance and then Father speaks. "He isn't. But if you multiply it by a hundred." He tilts his head and nods. "Then we might be getting somewhere. The cover story is we're running a private non-profit that organizes charity events and fundraisers for various causes. Your job is to help us set it up here locally and get the townspeople involved. We need you to extend the trust they have for you to us."

"So that's it? Tell people about you so they trust you?"

"For now." Father smiles at me.

"Fine. Will you answer a question for me, then?"

"What's your question?" Father asks.

"How did you find us?"

They exchange a glance.

"It wasn't hard to find the dealer where you bought the car," Mother says.

"And then it was only a matter of tracking two girls traveling alone together in a crap car across the country," Father says. "It wasn't hard. People tend to remember two pretty girls like you. Especially when you tell them the youngest has been *kidnapped*."

My jaw clenches at the word.

"But it's cute you tried."

There's more to the story than what they're telling me. They didn't track me across the country on their own. They're great at reading and working people, but they aren't technologically savvy and they aren't trackers. Someone they hired, maybe?

"We'll be in touch."

They leave. As they slide into the sleek black Mercedes parked across the street and pull away from the curb, all the tension leaves my body and I slump against the counter.

It's just like them to draw out the terror as long as they possibly can.

I can't let them get away with this. But what do I do?

I have to think, but it's so hard to form coherent thoughts when my heart is racing and my world is ending.

This whole thing . . . it isn't quite like them. Even with my involvement and the trust I've gained within the community, it will still have to be a quick con. Rushing makes people sloppy and that's when the cops swoop in. They taught me that. So why the rush? Why do they need money so quickly? To pay someone off? Someone scarier than them? They *have* developed some shady friends along the way, and it wouldn't surprise me to learn they owe someone a debt or that they've finally pissed the wrong person off.

They even came inside the shop and talked openly about their scheme. They never do that. Ever. They're always worried about bugs indoors—and not the creepy-crawly kind. See? Sloppy. But this time, I'll be the one swooping in, not the cops. If they're so rushed that they're hatching their nefarious plans here in the shop, I'll bug Ruby's shop myself.

The bell over the door jangles, and I start at the noise.

"Why didn't you tell me you and Jared had gone public?" It's Tabby. She's wearing a sundress and a white floppy hat with giant sunglasses.

"Um." My brain is still catching up with everything.

She moves toward me, taking off her hat and glasses and tossing them on the counter. "Why did I have to hear about you canoodling on the beach with Jared from Mrs. Olsen?"

I swallow and take a few quick seconds to pull myself together.

I can compartmentalize with the best of them.

Act normal.

"We were hardly canoodling. What does that word even mean anyway?"

Her eyes roll upward and she sighs. "You know, smooching, necking, snogging, petting—"

"Okay, there was absolutely no petting happening on the beach. Paige was there."

"So petting would have been on the table if she wasn't?"

"Petting in public is never on the table."

"Such a prude." She wrinkles her nose at me. "What are you doing tonight?"

"Um." I'm surprised at the subject change. "Don't you want to hear about Jared?"

"I get it." She shrugs. "You're in love. It's obvious."

I laugh and avoid eye contact while heat creeps up my face. "We're hardly in love. We aren't even officially dating."

"You're not even officially dating? What do you mean?"

"I mean we haven't even talked about that."

She sighs and shakes her head. "Men are so dumb sometimes."

"It's okay. We're just, you know, hanging out or whatever."

"Right." She snorts. "Like Ben and I were hanging out? Take it from someone who's been there. Get the man to commit before you give up your cookies."

I flush.

Her mouth pops open. "It's too late, isn't it? He already ate the cookies."

I can't help but laugh. "Amongst other things."

Her eyes nearly bug out of her head. "Did he eat the cookies with the milk?"

"Wait, what are we talking about here? I thought I understood your euphemisms but now I'm lost. What's the difference between the cookies and the milk?"

"If you have to ask, then there's no point in explaining it. So, are you free tonight or will you be too busy with the free cookie handouts?"

I have no idea. Jared hasn't said anything about hanging out tonight. He might not want to come over. We've already spent the last few nights and days together. What if he's sick of me?

When I don't immediately answer, Tabby talks into my silence. "Awesome. We're going out."

"We are?"

"Yep. I'll come by at six to get ready."

"Are we going to Ben's?"

"Hell no."

"What happened? Didn't you guys have a date?" I almost forgot about it, with all of the craziness of the last few days. Ben asked Tabby out on mocktail night and she had been excited to go on a real date with him.

"Dude." She holds up her hands. "Our date? Our first date? He took me bowling."

"What's wrong with bowling?"

"A better question would be what isn't wrong with bowling? I mean, for a first date, it's just not done."

"It's not?"

"No." She looks at me like I've got a bowling ball for a brain. "The food is terrible, it's loud, and you have to wear those shoes that don't go with anything and make you look like a clown."

"I guess that isn't so fun then."

"It's not. But it's okay. We're not fighting. After we went *bowling*," she grimaces, "he said he would take me somewhere nicer next time, but I'm making him work for it. Basically, he's wooing me and I'm being appropriately unavailable."

"Ah. Like in the wild. The male chases the female, and the female does some kind of dance ritual so he has to catch her."

"This isn't a dance ritual. It's more of a, you-deserve-to-suffer-for-being-such-an-asshole ritual."

"Well done."

Our conversation is cut short when some customers come in. Tabby lingers for a few minutes to chat when I'm not ringing up purchases or answering questions. Eventually, she leaves, promising to return around six.

Once the rush of shoppers dies down, I'm left alone again with thoughts of the parents and what I'm going to do. I run through our conversation in my head, trying to remember their exact words and motions. Was there anything I missed? Did they drop any hints about what they've been up to?

Other than this lame charity scam. They want to organize some kind of donation and take people's money, but it's got to be more than that. I wonder if there's a way I can gain some more insight about what they're planning.

Children's laughter filters in from behind the house.

When I peek out the back window, Mr. Bingel and the boys are in his backyard. The boys are running through the sprinklers, squealing and laughing, while Mr. Bingel sits in a lawn chair with a book on his lap, occasionally glancing up when the boys yell at him.

I smile. They look like they're having fun.

How did the parents know anything about Mr. Bingel and his circumstances? Have they spoken with him?

I leave the back door open so I can hear the bell above the shop door if anyone comes in.

"Hey, Mr. Bingel," I call over our shared fence. It's not a tall fence, maybe four feet. The white paint is chipped and peeling. His chair isn't far from me, only a few feet from the fence line.

He nods in my direction, as stoic as ever.

"Hi, Miss Ruby!" Gary calls out. Both boys wave in my direction, their dark hair soaked and dripping.

"Watch what I can do!" Gary proceeds to do a cartwheel through the water spurting out of the sprinkler, his legs flailing uncertainly in the air before he lands on wobbly feet.

"Nice job!" I call out. I stand there for a minute.

Mr. Bingel is giving me the silent treatment, again.

I can see I'll have to work the information out of him. "How have you been, Mr. Bingel?"

"Just fine, thank you."

And we drop back into silence. "I've been fine, thanks for asking."

He scowls.

"The shop's been busy," I continue. "Lots of new people. Mostly tourists here for the summer."

We're quiet again for a minute, but the boys shrieking and playing in the background help ease the silence.

Drawing conversation from Mr. Bingel— without Jared present—is like trying to conjure a master key for the Federal Reserve out of thin air. But I'm not going to let it stand in my way.

Since beating around the bush with small talk isn't working, I jump right to it. I need to get to the point before more customers show up at the shop.

"My aunt and uncle are in town for a bit. They mentioned meeting someone older with two small children, and I thought it might be you. Do you remember meeting them? They're both good-looking, midforties. She has dark hair and he looks sort of like a younger Liam Neeson."

"Oh, yes. Leah and David."

Bingo. "So you've met."

"They came over to introduce themselves the other day and invited me to help with their charity project."

"That's so . . . generous of them. So like them." The words are like dirt in my mouth. "They're really involved in their causes." I notice his word choice. They invited him to help. Classic con move, making someone feel like they're needed.

"It was interesting. I'd never heard of a nonprofit that acts as a clearinghouse for other charities, raising money for local and national causes all at once. But they told me their real money goes to the injured veteran's project."

For a second I think I might lose my cool, but I manage to rein it in.

The scam itself is pretty disgusting, but even more concerning is how much they know.

They know about Mr. Bingel's son, how he died in the military, and they're using it against him.

Of course they are.

Why do I have to be related to them? They're going to prey on the kindness of the people of Castle Cove. I can see it now. They have set it up perfectly. They can pick and choose who to target and how to sock them right where it hurts the most, right where they care. With their expensive clothes and charming personalities—trotted out whenever it's advantageous to them—they'll have everyone opening their wallets in no time at all.

With my assistance.

"Wow," I say. "That's so cool."

I doubt there's any more information I can glean from him, and I can't continue this line of conversation without punching something, so I change the subject to the weather and the boys and what they'll be doing over summer break.

When the bell of the shop door rings in the distance, I make my excuses and hustle back. I'm not sure what to do with this new information, but I know I can't let them get away with this.

CHAPTER FOUR

Tabby shows up right before six. I don't tell Paige what I've discovered. The more I can keep her out of this whole mess, the better. She's already getting worn down with everything that happened the other night, and since Naomi left, she's only going to get worse with nothing else to distract her. Keeping things as normal as possible is my aim. *Keep Paige safe.*

That's why I wait until she's in the bathroom to hide a listening device at the front counter. Now I just have to make sure the next time the parents show up that it's on and they're speaking in its general vicinity. It won't help me thwart their plans, but it could make for insurance against a double cross later.

I get the bug positioned below the lip of the cash register just as Tabby arrives armed with a tool kit of makeup, hair-styling products, and clothes.

She insists on fixing my hair first, taking her time and styling it into loose curls that hang around my shoulders. Then she does my makeup.

"Are we going somewhere fancy?" I ask when she's throwing dresses at me. They aren't necessarily fancy dresses, more like sundresses, but still.

"Maybe." Her smile is fleeting and coy. "You'll need flat shoes. Something comfortable." She bends over in the closet, mumbling to herself and shoving shoes around.

"What aren't you telling me?" She's obviously hiding something. I'm all glamoured up, while she's still in her yoga pants and a ponytail.

"Are you coming with me to the Founders' Day Parade this weekend?"

"Are you changing the subject?"

"This is important, Ruby." She stands and faces me, her hands on her hips. "There's competitions. They have races and games and I need a teammate I can count on."

Being Tabby's teammate for a competition is asking for trouble. It would be like partnering with a professional athlete for an Olympic event. Not that Tabby has the skills of a professional athlete, merely the expectations.

"What about Troy?" I ask.

"Troy sucks at everything. He loses on purpose because he likes to make me angry. Please, Ruby? Say you'll be my date?" She presses her hands together.

"Um, well." Now is a good time to work on the task assigned to me. Even though the thought still makes me sick. "I have family in town, so I'll have to check and see. I might be busy."

"What? What family?"

"Remember how I told you last week that my aunt and uncle came through town and I missed them?" My excuse for a maître d' at a restaurant calling me Charlotte is actually coming in handy right now.

"Right, we saw a guy that worked at their hotel or whatever."

"Well, they came back. And I think they're staying a little longer this time."

"Oh good, I'll be able to meet them."

"Maybe." I shrug it off like it's no big deal even though it is and I won't be able to avoid it forever. Kill me now.

"Well either way, if they're here, then they should come to the parade, too. I'm sure they wouldn't preclude you from all the super-fun activities."

"I'll try to convince them. Plus I'll be your teammate if you explain to me why I'm all dressed up and you look like you're going to bed."

The doorbell rings. She grins and turns back to sorting through my shoes.

"Tabby." I inject my voice with warning.

She doesn't say anything, instead handing me a pair of flat silver sandals.

"Tabby."

"Okay, so we wanted to surprise you."

"What kind of surprise?"

Before she can answer, Paige is at the bedroom door. "Jared is here. There's a fancy car out front."

"What did you guys do?"

Tabby raises her hands in surrender. "I didn't do anything. This was all Jared. Come on. I want to see his face when he sees you."

I swallow and follow her out the door. I haven't talked to him since this morning, when he met the parents. I know he's going to ask about them, about why I didn't mention them before. It's not like I've never lied to Jared, but this feels bigger, scarier. Like if all my other lies are little sand dunes, this lie is Everest.

But then he's there, at the bottom of the stairs waiting for me.

We make eye contact and his face lights up.

Tabby sighs behind me. "So romantic."

"What are we doing?" I ask when I reach the bottom of the steps.

Jared takes my hand, pressing a gentle kiss to my palm. "It's a surprise."

His clothes are a bit more casual than mine, dark jeans and a formfitting blue Henley that's pushed up at the sleeves, drawing my attention to his forearms.

"I'll be here with Paige." Tabby pushes us in the direction of the front door. "You kids have fun!" Then she shuts the door on us.

I frown and look down at myself. "Should I be bringing more than this?" All I have are the clothes on my back and the flat, strappy sandals still in my hands.

"You're perfect just like that."

The car out front is a black town car.

"What is this?"

"This is our ride." He opens the back door so I can slide in. The interior is all dark leather seats, and a partition closes us off from the driver.

"You're really not going to tell me where we're going?"

He slides in after me and shuts the door. "Nope. Not yet. But you'll figure it out soon enough. Drink?" He opens a bag on the seat next to him and pulls out a bottle of champagne as the car pulls away from the curb.

"Oh, wow," I say. "This is . . ."

His lips purse. "It's too much, isn't it?"

"It's a little overwhelming." I can't believe he did all of this for me.

"I wanted to do something special. We haven't gone on a real date, but we've been . . ." The pink spreading up his neck is cute. "You know."

I laugh. "Oh, I know. But seriously, this isn't necessary. No need to woo when you've already got access to the goods."

"But that's just it, I want to woo you. I should have wooed you before."

"You do?"

"Of course." He says it like it's a no-brainer.

But it's not. Not every guy, or maybe even most guys, would go through all this trouble.

"I like wooing," I say after a few beats.

"Do you? So I'm doing a good job?"

"Yeah. I could use a little more, though."

"Like what?"

I grab the front of his shirt and pull him closer. "I'll show you."

With his lips on mine, I forget about the town car and the champagne and wherever we're heading. All that exists for a few blissful moments is the puff of his breath on my lips and the heat of his body against mine.

A knock rattles us apart. The car has come to a stop. Pulling back from Jared, I glance out the window.

We're at the docks next to the pier. Boats and yachts bob along the water.

"Come on." Jared opens the door and gets out before turning to take my hand. Then he reaches into the car and grabs a black bag from the floor.

He holds my hand as we walk down the pier, linking his fingers through mine. Near the end of the dock, he stops and motions to one of the yachts.

"Here we are."

I stare at the shiny white boat. "Is this your boat?"

"No. I rented it. I thought it would be fun to take it out and eat dinner out in the bay under the stars. Was this a bad idea? I know you had a fear of the water before, but maybe being on the water will be a little different than swimming in it, and I thought it might be fun."

I gape at him. "This is . . . crazy. Amazing. Jared, this must have cost a fortune."

He shrugs. "Not really." His grin is infectious.

He assists me from the dock onto the boat. Then we spend some time looking around and he shows me where everything is. The boat is big, but small enough to be manned by one person. There's a cabin sunk into the middle with a bed, small shower and kitchenette. The deck is sleek and white with cushioned seats lining the interior.

We get distracted by the bed, and by the time we emerge from the cabin, the sun is setting and our clothes are rumpled from being thrown on the floor.

Jared only has to push a few buttons to bring up the anchor and start the engines, and then he's spinning the white-leather-lined steering wheel like he's been driving a boat his whole life.

"You know how to drive this thing?"

"I've taken some boats out a time or two." He winks at me. "Don't be nervous, we aren't going far."

He steers us away from the pier and out onto the bay.

He stops before we get out onto the open ocean, cutting the motor and then dropping the anchor. We're still within the curve of the cove, but far enough away to see the lights of Castle Cove twinkling against the dark span of land while the stars wink into existence above us.

It's just the two of us, gently rocking amongst the waves and the stars.

"This is so pretty."

"I brought you something."

He disappears inside the cabin and returns with a basket.

"What's this?"

"Dinner. I hope you're hungry."

He pulls out some blankets and pillows from under a cushioned seat and we make a picnic on the deck. Out of the basket come plates, utensils, napkins and then a few containers full of food.

"I wasn't sure what kind of pasta you liked, so I got a few options."

"You brought me pasta?"

"And wine." He grins.

"You remembered." Hell, I barely remembered until now. He asked what my favorite food was when we were meandering around the swap meet, and I told him Italian.

"You can never go wrong with carbs and wine," he says, repeating my words back to me from the weekend before.

There's a seafood pasta with mussels in a white wine sauce, and another pasta smothered in red vodka sauce. There's a salad, bread sticks, a nice bottle of wine, and tiramisu for dessert.

Once we've eaten, I collapse back on the pillows, stuffed. "I think I'm going to have a food baby."

"There's more."

"If I eat anything else, I will puke."

"It's not food. I brought something else for you. Another surprise."

"There's more?" I sit up.

"Just wait until you see this." He's way too excited and it's way too cute.

Maybe whatever he brought involves me and him naked on this deck.

He pushes a button that pulls up one of the sails in front of us.

Then he grabs a black square object from under one of the chairs and sets it up on a ledge behind us.

There's the click of a few buttons and then an image flickers onto the sail in front of me.

I gasp. "It's a movie." And not just any movie. I laugh out loud as the opening credits to *Calamity Jane* scroll by.

"Do you remember everything?"

"I remember everything you say." He sits next to me, grinning like a fool, and I can't control myself. I lean into him, peppering his face with kisses.

"Keep this up and we'll be doing this every night," he says when my kisses move down his neck.

I lift my lips from his skin long enough to say, "If I eat like that every night, I'll get so big you won't be able to move me from this boat ever again."

"That problem is easily solved." His arms are around me, one thumb running slow circles on my waist, sending sparks through my whole body. "I'll help you burn some of those extra calories."

"Will you?" I swing one leg over him, straddling his waist.

His hands tighten around me. "It'll be a real hardship."

I laugh, the sound a throaty chuckle around my growing need. I cup his face in my hands and stare down at him for a second.

I wish I could keep him.

Shoving the thought aside, I tilt my head and kiss him until everything else disappears.

The movie is halfway over when we finally come up for air.

We snuggle on the deck, watching the rest of the movie. Jared won't stop touching me. Our fingers play and twine together. His hand brushes my hair, my cheek, my bare thigh. I listen to the steady beat of his heart under my head as it rests on his chest.

"I wish we could stay here forever," I say on a sigh.

"We might get scurvy."

I laugh. "This isn't exactly the high seas."

We're quiet for a minute, the silence comfortable. Doris Day is onscreen, singing that her heart is an open door.

I couldn't have planned a more perfect night.

"Jared." My voice is thick with emotion I can't hide. "Thank you."

His arm tightens around me. "What are you thanking me for?"

"Dinner. This." I motion to everything around us. "For taking care of me and Paige all the time. I don't know why you do it."

"I care about you. And Paige."

I lift my head and rest my chin on his chest so I can see him. "I know." I just can't understand why.

His eyes find mine in the dim light, so steady and reassuring. "I meant what I said before, about putting some money aside for Paige for college. Have you thought about it?"

I swallow and avert my gaze. I don't want to talk about money right now. "I have." Another thought strikes me. "Can I ask you about something?"

"Of course."

"Can you . . . if anything ever happened to me, would you look after Paige?"

"If anything ever happened to you? Why would something happen to you?" He brushes a strand of hair back from my face, his fingers brushing my cheek, his eyes narrowing in concern.

"Nothing's going to happen," I reassure him. "Well, nothing that I know of. It's just one of those things, you know, to think about. Worry about. If something happens to me, I don't want Paige to be alone. You can't count on being around forever."

"I know." He does. After another moment he nods. "I promise. If anything happens to you, I'll do whatever I can for Paige."

I relax into him for a second. "Thank you."

One of his fingers rubs against my arm, the gentle pressure both soothing and arousing. "I want to ask you something, but I don't want to pressure you. I know you've been a bit anxious about any kind of commitment, but I like you." One corner of his lips twitches downward and his arm tenses against me, the only signs of his nerves.

I consider teasing him, then decide to put him out of his misery. "I like you, too."

"I like you a lot, and I hope you'll consider being with me. Officially."

My heart beats faster in my chest. I lift up the thin blanket covering us, exposing our intertwined naked bodies. "I'm not sure if it gets more official than this."

He laughs and gives me a squeeze. "You know what I mean."

"Are you saying you *like* me, like me? Like you wanna go steady and give me your class ring and letterman jacket?"

He laughs and some of the tension runs out of him. "I would hope it's obvious. And yes I *like* you, like you. You can wear my letterman jacket anytime, as long as that's all you're wearing." His smile is brief but blinding, his eyes smoldering.

I can't say no right now, even though I should. I shouldn't be doing anything the parents are encouraging, but I can't help it. I want him too much.

"Of course." I lean up and press a gentle kiss to his lips.

"Is that a yes?"

"Yes."

His arms tighten around me. "Well thank god for that. Does this mean I get to kiss you in public?"

I laugh. I know he's thinking about the other day at the beach. "I don't know." It's not that I'm opposed to public displays of affection, I just don't want the parents to get any sense of the intimacy I feel with Jared. I know they're already suspicious of his financial status because of the house, and I can't stop them from digging into his life, but I don't need to give them any more reasons to use him against me.

"You don't want people to know we're together?"

"It's not, it's just . . . I don't know. As long as you don't try to make out with me in the town square in front of Mrs. Olsen and everyone, it's fine."

"I would never do such a thing. In front of Mrs. Olsen, it's light groping only, absolutely no making out. Wouldn't want her to get the wrong idea."

I laugh and smack him on the arm.

We're silent for a moment, listening to the sound of the waves and the wind against the sails.

"Can I kiss you in front of your aunt and uncle?"

I force myself not to tense. I knew he would bring them up, eventually. "Of course."

"You never mentioned them." His voice isn't accusatory. At all. But it should be.

And that thought makes me feel a thousand times guiltier than I already am.

How can I explain them? Their wealth? The fact that Paige and I have struggled, yet we didn't turn to them for help? How can I do all that while still doing what they asked and convincing him of their con? More lies. More deception.

"We had a bit of a falling out, but they're trying to make amends."

"What happened?" His voice is layered with concern and care. For me. I don't deserve it. Not for these lies.

I swallow back the guilt and force the false words out of my mouth. I have to keep up the pretense if Paige and I are going to get out of this mess.

"They've always been really great to Paige and me, especially after our parents died. But I needed to stand on my own. You know?"

"Why didn't they take custody of Paige?"

"Their work keeps them really busy, and they travel a lot. All over the country. They would have taken Paige. They offered to stop working for their charity organization, but I couldn't ask them to do that. It means so much to them to help so many people."

Gag. But it's convincing, isn't it? I can't help but be a little proud of how believable my lies are while simultaneously feeling like a piece of garbage covered in dog turds.

"Hmm." He acknowledges my words with just a murmur.

"Are you going to the Founders' Day Parade?" I have to change the subject before he asks any more questions about them.

"Yeah. I have to. We ride in the procession with the mayor and then we have to follow him around most of the day. Security." He shakes his head.

"It's not fun?"

"It's okay, but completely unnecessary. There's no gunman waiting on the grassy knoll in Castle Cove. It's more of a formality than anything. But someone has to do it. Normally the chief covers it, but this year he's going to dress as Santa for the Christmas float."

"Christmas float? It's June."

"Yeah. You don't have to explain to me how crazy this place is. But the people love it and he insisted. I think he's got a bit of short-timer syndrome going on. He's retiring in a few years." He chuckles. "We had some extra budget money for supplies and he bought some crazy spy equipment."

I laugh. "Spy equipment? Like what?"

"GPS trackers, recording devices that look like everyday items—like pens and a pair of glasses. He even got a neodymium magnet."

"Is he planning on robbing a bank?"

Jared's hand, which had been gently moving up and down the outside of my arm, stops suddenly.

"How did you know neodymium is used on safes?"

"Oh." I laugh it off. "I think I saw it in a movie once."

Shit. How did I let that slip? Jared makes me feel too comfortable when I should be on guard. At least he seems to buy my excuse because his hand starts moving in gentle circles again.

I've actually never had cause to use one, but I looked into it, once. There was a document safe the parents had, a small one, and it was always around when I was growing up. I don't know what was in it, but it moved with us everywhere and the parents would always store it under their bed. I never had a chance to try and open it, though.

"I didn't have the heart to tell the chief you can't use GPS on people without a warrant. And the magnet is dangerous, especially around electronics. It can damage other magnetic devices like credit cards, watches, whatever even from a distance. I had him lock the items up downstairs in the archives. We'll probably never even use them. I can't even imagine how much he spent on all that stuff."

We're quiet, watching the movie for a minute before I speak again. "I might see you at the parade. Tabby wants me on her team for some kind of game thing."

"You might regret agreeing to that."

"I've seen her play games, and I already have regrets."

"I'd save you from her crazy, but we're way too understaffed for an event like this. I can meet up with you after, though."

"Can I ask you something?"

"Sure."

"Why do you work if you don't have to?"

He's quiet for a moment, considering my words while his thumb draws slow circles on my arm. "If I didn't have something to keep me busy, I think I'd lose my mind."

"I can see that."

He sighs a little. "The distraction has really helped me deal with my parents' deaths. But you've helped, too. I don't feel so . . . guilty anymore."

"Guilty? Why would you feel guilty?"

He doesn't speak for a moment, and I can feel him gathering his thoughts. It's in the sudden tension of his arms, the increased thumping of his heart against me.

"I should have been here. I missed so much because I had to move to a bigger city, a bigger life. If I hadn't left . . ."

"You don't know that you could have stopped what happened to them. It was an accident, no one's fault, except maybe the other driver."

He shrugs. "Maybe they would still be gone. Maybe not. But I would have had more time with them. I was always too busy. I couldn't even keep a relationship alive with someone who lived in the same town, let alone remember to call my mom on Sundays or visit over the holidays. I forgot what was really important until it was too late." There's a slight pressure on the top of my head, like he's brushing his lips against my hair. "I won't forget it ever again."

It makes sense to me now. Why he doesn't want to use their money, why he cares so much for the people in this town—which now includes Paige and myself.

And I'm conning him.

CHAPTER FIVE

We go to breakfast at Stella's, the diner in Castle Cove, still wearing rumpled clothing from the night before, but we don't care.

He drops me off at Ruby's midmorning, walking me to the door and kissing me goodbye on the porch. Tabby sticks her head out and heckles us, but we just laugh. He has to go to work, and so do I.

Once he leaves, I thank Tabby for staying with Paige, and then once she's gone, I shower and open the shop.

Paige hangs out and helps for a while until she gets bored and goes to play with the boys next door in Mr. Bingel's sprinklers.

It would all be perfectly domestic if it weren't for the threat of our parents looming over everything.

As if my very thoughts conjure them, they show up in the shop.

They're still dressed impeccably, looking fresh even in the summer heat, always as smooth as ice.

"Hello, Daughter dear," Mother says.

Today, there's no looking around or backhanded compliments. However, the silver lining to their appearance is that they walk right up to the counter where I'm standing, finishing up the day's accounts—and thumbing on the listening device below the register.

"We have another assignment for you," Father says.

I don't say anything. I just wait for them to spit it out.

"It's about your boyfriend. Deputy Reeves, I believe?" Mother's eyes are focused on me, waiting for my reaction to her words.

I don't move, keeping my expression blank.

They don't waste any time.

"I'm not sure if you know this, honey, but it turns out lover boy is better off than you might think." Father's voice is infused with an exaggerated measure of shock.

He knows I know, as I'm sure they've known since the first night at his house.

Mother is still scrutinizing my face, weighing my expressions against her words. "I knew there was more to his story when I saw his house. Maintenance alone must be rather pricey. As it turns out, he inherited quite a bit when his parents died. And since you're so cozy and all, it'll be a snap for you to get us his account information."

Blood rushes from my head, but I refuse to show any kind of emotional response.

This is all my fault. If only I hadn't come to Castle Cove. If only I hadn't pretended to be Ruby. If only I hadn't gotten close to Jared.

"Are you dropping the charity con then to go after a bigger fish?" I ask. Come on, come on, admit to the whole thing while my little friend with the big ears listens . . .

"No," Mother says.

I pause. "You want to run a double con? You always told me that was a bad idea."

Father rolls his eyes and shakes his head at me. "We know what we're doing. No one will suspect anything until it's too late. We won't touch your boyfriend's money until after the big con is done. We'll be long gone before anyone notices anything missing."

Mother agrees. "We thought of making you do more work than this, you know, something really hard since you ran away with our money and daughter and all that, but we decided to be nice to you. This one time. Get us his account information and his password, and you and Paige are free to go."

My heart thumps dully in my chest. This is the choice they've presented? Screw over Jared? How could I? After everything . . .

"As an added incentive." Father pulls a folded paper out of his jacket and holds it out to me.

I don't necessarily want to approach him, but I also don't want him to see my trepidation. Don't show any weakness.

I force my buttery legs to move toward him and pluck the paper from his grasp.

"What is this?" I ask, my eyes running over the words. It's a legal document, and at first I can't make sense of what I'm reading. Would they . . .

"We haven't signed it yet, but if you do this," Father says, "your debt to us will be paid and we'll sign Paige over to you. Fully and legally."

I can't process it. They must want this money very badly to give me this kind of leverage. Or maybe they really don't care, but they know I do and that's why they are dangling such a carrot in front of me. They know nothing would entice me more.

A little, sickening voice whispers in my mind. *He doesn't want the money anyway.* He's already trying to give some of it to Paige for school. I would be doing him a favor.

I lower the paper and lock eyes with Father. Then I nod, just once.

"Good girl." Mother pats me on the hand like I'm a child who's done something to be proud of. "This will be easy for you. After all, you've done it before. Don't feel bad about this man. He's not one of us. He never will be. I can tell you like him, but someday you'll find someone better. It was the same for your father and I."

They exchange a heated look and I want to barf.

I've heard bits and pieces of their story before. Mother always said Father saved her. From what I've been able to gather, her parents—my grandparents—were rather well-off. They met when Father was conning them. When Mother discovered what he was about, instead of turning him in, she joined up with him.

For all of their faults and their inability to care about anyone but themselves, they do seem to love each other. It was something I almost envied about them, their relationship. As horrible as they've been to me, and as negligent as they've been to Paige, they've never treated each other badly.

Before they leave out the front door, Father stops and looks me straight in the face. "Don't try to leave. If you do, we'll find you, but not after we finish our work here."

They leave and I stare at the wall in front of me for a minute, not really seeing anything.

"You can't do that," Paige says from behind me.

I whip my head in her direction, her voice knocking me out of my stupor.

She's still in her swimsuit, the beach towel Jared gave her covering her thin, dripping frame.

"We can't do this," she repeats.

I nod. "I know."

She shakes her head, her expression nearly as lost as I feel at the moment.

"I'll come up with a plan."

I hope.

~*~

The following Saturday, the Founders' Day Parade starts bright and early at eight o'clock.

Paige is going to walk down to Main Street with Mr. Bingel and the boys, so she sleeps until seven thirty.

I am not so lucky.

Tabby doesn't give me any leeway. She's at the door right at seven because we have to find the best place to sit for the parade.

"Finding a good spot is the most important part," Tabby says as we're walking from Ruby's to Main Street. "You need to find somewhere you can see all the floats. It's gotta be close to the hot cocoa stand and not too far from the bathrooms. But not too close either, because, ew."

She brought chairs we can carry on our backs and a small cooler with water and snacks.

It's warm and slightly humid outside, even in the early morning hours. Tabby told me to wear something comfortable, something I could run in — which is a bit scary, but she's only referring to the competitions she wants me to do with her, although that thought is frightening in and of itself.

"Did your aunt and uncle decide to come?" Tabby asks.

"They said they'd try to make it, so we might see them there. They have some work stuff going on." I shrug it off.

I have no idea what they're up to. I've been waiting for them to appear at the shop and demand the account information, but they've been MIA since they leveled me with their task. All a part of their plan, surely. Make me anxious and stressed while they hover over me like some kind of demonic specters.

They can't know that I bugged Ruby's. Unless that's why they're now avoiding the shop?

In addition to planting the bugs, I've spent the momentary reprieve figuring out where they're staying—in one of the priciest parts of town, of course—and searching for what they did with my car. I still haven't found it. Whatever they did with it, they aren't keeping it at their new place. The only car there, when I scoped it out under cover of darkness, was the black Mercedes.

"How long does the parade last?" I ask.

"Like three hours."

"Seriously? That long? How many floats can there be?"

"Well, you know, the middle school band, the high school band, the cheerleading and drill teams, the local radio station, the Girl Scouts, the Boy Scouts, some local businesses, law enforcement, the mayor . . . you get the picture. And then afterward is the Founders' Day Festival, and at night, there's music and dancing in the park."

"This is going to be a long day."

"At least you have something to look forward to: dancing in Jared's arms under the stars."

I tuck my head to hide my smile.

I've seen Jared every day this week. Sometimes it's for dinner, and sometimes he pops in for lunch during his work shift. He even brought me breakfast the other day when he went out for his morning run.

I haven't done anything about the parents' most recent demands. How can I? They didn't give me a timeline—probably on purpose to make the waiting even crueler—but I know before too long they're going to show up again, expecting me to hand over Jared's account information.

They have to. We don't have much time to finish this con before Ruby gets back.

My stomach twists when I think about actually going through with it. Are there other options? If I say no . . . what will they do? There has to be another choice, something I haven't yet thought of.

We haven't been to his house all week, he always comes over to Ruby's, so it's not like I've had much opportunity anyway.

Once we reach the main road, there are already people taking up spots along the sidewalk, even though we're nearly an hour early.

It takes a few minutes for Tabby to find the perfect area to sit, and we end up smooshed in between a few elderly people in their wheelchairs on one side and a family with young kids on the other. I set up the chairs while Tabby goes to the hot cocoa stand for drinks.

While I'm saving our spots, Mrs. Olsen walks by wearing a cat-covered T-shirt, still pushing Miss Viola around even though we all know the woman can walk just fine, and Judge Ramsey and his wife wave at me from across the street.

It's weird how comfortable it feels, talking and waving, being a part of a community. At the same time, my eyes are continually scanning the crowd for two faces I absolutely do not want to see amongst the children and revelers and vendors walking around selling hats, T-shirts, and giant stuffed animals. But I don't see them, only the happy, quirky people of Castle Cove.

A shadow stops right next to me, unmoving. Tabby, holding a cup of hot cocoa in each hand, staring into the distance with a blank face.

"Tabby?"

Her eyes flick toward me but she doesn't move.

"Are you okay?"

"I just saw . . ." She shakes her head. Her mouth opens but nothing comes out. Then her mouth closes.

Standing, I take the cups from her and put them down in the cup holders on our chairs. I touch her arm and she startles. "What did you see?"

I expect her to say something terrible. Someone was crushed by a runaway float, maybe stung to death by bees, or *Sharknado* is now a reality and a great white is looming on the horizon.

"I saw—Troy. Making out with—Eleanor." Her sentence is broken, like she can barely speak the words.

I laugh, relaxing. "Is that it? I thought you saw something truly horrible."

"No, you don't understand, they were like totally sucking face. It was worse than horrible."

"Eleanor's not that bad."

"She's not. But I saw my brother's tongue in her mouth. I've been scarred for life." She plops down in her chair, still grimacing, and I sit next to her.

"Why don't you seem surprised?" She turns toward me, lips pursed, eyes narrowed.

"I'm not."

"Did you have a psychic vision about this? Because if so, being a clairvoyant isn't as cool as I thought it would be."

"Um . . ." I scratch the back of my head. "Sort of. It came up a couple weeks ago."

She stares at me, her eyes wide and unblinking. "You knew?"

"I did. I'm sorry I didn't tell you, but it wasn't really my place."

She slumps. "I know. I'm not mad at you. It's just—I can't believe it."

"Is it really so hard to believe? He's single, she's single. There's not many of those in our age range nearby."

"Yeah but she's just so . . . bland."

"Tabby!"

"I don't mean to sound rude, it's just that I've known her for like ten years, and other than knowing where she works and that she must like books, I literally know nothing about her."

"Have you ever tried to get to know her?"

"Sure," she waves a hand, "years ago. I invited her to karaoke night at Ben's and she acted like I'd invited her to sample some herpes-infested cakes."

I laugh. "I'm sure she didn't react that badly."

"No, really. She mumbled something incoherent and ran away from me as soon as she could."

"She's obviously shy. Maybe karaoke isn't her thing. She came to trivia night, remember?"

She shrugs. "She didn't say much then either."

"You should give her another chance."

"I just don't want to see her making out with my brother again." Her mouth twists. "Yuck. That is an image I wish I could scrub from my brain."

The parade starts, and Tabby is distracted by the first float. It's a giant rooster made by the local high school.

"That's the school mascot." Tabby leans over to tell me. "A rooster. We're literally the Castle Cove Cocks."

I choke on a laugh and we cheer and clap with the rest of the town as various groups and organizations march by.

The crowd gets really excited when the mayor cruises down the street in a bright-red convertible, flanked on all sides by police cruisers. The car in the rear has its windows down and I hear the catcalls before I see Jared. I'm not surprised every female in his radius is whistling at him. The man makes panties melt all over town. Even if they are mostly granny panties.

When the car reaches us, it rolls to a complete stop.

Jared jumps out of the passenger seat, strolling over to where Tabby and I are sitting. He looks amazing in his perfectly pressed police uniform, as usual.

"What are you—?"

He doesn't let me finish my sentence.

He reaches down, grabs my hand, and pulls me to my feet. Then he leans down and kisses me, right there on Main Street in front of the entire town.

I should protest, but once his mouth hits mine it's like every time he touches me—I melt into him like butter on hot pavement.

After a moment, he releases me, giving me a crooked grin and squeezing my hand. "I know I said I wouldn't kiss you in front of everyone, but . . . I lied." He winks before jogging back to the patrol car.

I watch the car drive slowly away before regaining my senses.

People are still clapping and whistling.

I glance around and wave a bit awkwardly. Through the smiling crowd, I spot Father's profile. There's a shift in the line of bodies and he disappears. Even though I keep scanning for another minute, it's no use. He's vanished.

"That was hot," Tabby says next to me, fanning herself with one hand. "Way better than watching my brother. Girl, he is so into you."

I smile, but inwardly, the euphoria of his blatant display of affection is sinking into a yawning pit in my stomach.

It's not that I don't want him to be into me. But I can't help but worry about the fallout.

What have I gotten myself into?

Worse, what have I gotten Jared into?

CHAPTER SIX

"I can't believe he teamed up with her," Tabby grumbles as she stretches in the grass, warming up like we're about to run a marathon.

We're in the park, in a large grassy expanse where the games have been set up. We're waiting for the first event to begin, which is the potato sack race.

"It's no big deal."

"It is a big deal. He never wanted to be on my team. I had to threaten him with bodily harm and even then he complained the whole time. But Eleanor sticks her tongue down his throat once and he says yes?"

"Well, you're a little . . ."

"Fun?" she offers. "Exciting? Best teammate ever?"

"I was going to say controlling and competitive, but those work, too."

"Aw, you're such a good friend, Ruby." She ceases her stretching and points at me. "Now get in that sack because you're going first. And you better not screw this up, because if they beat us, we can never speak again ever."

"Right."

The potato sack race is done relay style, the starting line about fifty feet from where Tabby and the other partners will wait. I have to hop over to Tabby and then give her my sack so she can hop back to the starting line to win the race.

"Good luck. Don't let me down." She claps me on the back before jogging over to where the second line has been drawn.

Holding my sack up to my waist, I glance down the line of participants. Mr. Godfrey is next to me; his partner is Mrs. Olsen. She's haranguing Tabby about wearing sunblock, her voice carrying across the field.

On the other side of him amongst others are Mrs. Hale, Troy, and Mr. Newsome.

Miss Viola is running the show, still in her unnecessary wheelchair. She's sitting at the end of the starting line with some kind of starting pistol.

I really hope someone made sure it isn't a real gun.

There's quiet down the line when Miss Viola pulls out a megaphone. She calls a countdown. When she pulls the trigger, we all jolt into action. I hop as fast as I can across the grass in my sack. It's harder than I thought it would be. Teammates and spectators are shouting alike but I'm focused on getting to Tabby without screwing up so she doesn't murder me.

Miss Viola yells something into the megaphone, but the resulting screech makes the words indecipherable. I glance her way. Someone has stopped to talk to her, bending slightly over her wheelchair. Their back is to me but the sleek dark hair pulled back in a chignon is unmistakable. Mother. Miss Viola smiles and pats her hand and Mother hands her something small. Maybe a business card. I can't tell from my vantage point. I'm straining, trying to see, and since I'm not paying attention to what I'm doing, my hop falters.

The misstep causes me to trip over the bottom seam of the burlap sack and down I go, tumbling to the ground.

Thank god it's grassy. I don't injure myself too badly—except for my pride. Tabby yells something at me, and while I can't quite make out what she's saying, it doesn't sound like words of encouragement. I pull myself back up and jump over to her.

She practically pushes me out of the sack before throwing herself inside of it and leaping away.

I'm not too concerned about the sack race or Tabby's temper anymore, though. I scan the nearby crowd, looking for Mother. Miss Viola is talking to someone else now, Mother nowhere in sight.

I try to shake it off, but I can't stop. Are they here? Will I have to deal with them today?

What did she say to Miss Viola? I'm going to have to find out.

I shove the parents out of my mind as Tabby hops like a demented gazelle across the finish line.

Miss Viola has her megaphone still in her hand. She pulls it up to her mouth. "The winners are Troy and Eleanor."

"No!" Tabby's yell echoes over the lawn of people.

I almost don't want to walk over there. She's going to kill me.

Troy is triumphant and Eleanor is smiling, but the motion is pinched. Her hand rubs her left side and she's watching Tabby.

"Calm your tits, Tabby, there's three more events," Miss Viola says into the megaphone, her voice booming over the park.

Three more events?

Tabby's mouth firms into a thin line and she stalks in my direction.

Oh, boy.

"We still have a chance," she says when we reach each other in the middle of the field. She doesn't seem angry, more determined. "The next event is the water balloon squat. We don't have to get first place. If we just beat Troy and Eleanor, I'll be happy."

"Really?"

"Well, I'd be happier if we beat everyone, but I'll settle for beating my brother because you're obviously a bit special." She pats me on the shoulder twice. And not lightly.

"Hey."

"If I'd known Eleanor could move like that, I would have had *her* on my team."

"Hey!"

"What? You suck, Ruby. And did you see Mrs. Ramsey? She totally pulled one leg out early. That bitch is going to get it."

I laugh. "Mrs. Ramsey is like the sweetest woman in the world."

"Whatever. She's still a damn cheater."

Miss Viola gets back on the megaphone and calls for everyone to line up again. Behind her, some guys are pulling bins full of water balloons to the starting line.

As they line up the balloon bins, Tabby explains the process.

For this event, we have to hold the water balloon between our thighs and walk—or waddle— with it all the way to the other line where there's an empty bucket we have to put them in. We get points for each balloon we get into the new bucket without dropping or breaking it, and an extra five points if we get all the balloons transferred first. Oh, and we can't use our hands.

"We're going to kick ass," Tabby says.

"We're going to look ridiculous."

"I know your thighs have been getting a workout lately." Tabby nudges me with her shoulder.

I groan. "You're worse than your brother."

"Now that's just cruel, Ruby. Why would you say such a thing? I'm going first this time."

"I have no problem with that."

We line up again; this time we're both on the same side. As soon as Tabby gets her balloon in the other bucket, I can start my way over and then she'll have to run back to get her next balloon. There are ten balloons total to move from one side to the other.

Miss Viola is back on the megaphone, yelling at us to get ready, set and go.

Tabby takes off like a penguin on speed, the balloon squeezed between her legs.

They all look so funny, waddling across. Mrs. Ramsey loses her balloon somewhere in the middle and laughs so hard she can hardly get back up. The only people not laughing are Tabby and Eleanor. They are like women on a mission, their feet shuffling while they eye each other across the field.

Not wanting to let Tabby down, as soon as she plops her balloon in the bucket, I'm waddling after her. It's harder than you might think to hold a wiggly, water-filled balloon between your legs, and I probably look like an idiot—everyone else does— but I know I'm doing good when Tabby runs past me, slapping me a high five on her way back to the starting point to get another balloon.

It takes a few seconds of positioning to get the balloon to drop into the second bucket—you basically have to crouch like you're pooping, but I get it done without incident. As I'm jogging back, I pass Tabby again. She's grinning like a madwoman, and I know why.

"Hurry up, you're going to make us lose!" shouts Eleanor.

I don't think I've ever heard her speak louder than a murmur, but she's giving it to Troy pretty good and Tabby is loving every second of it.

It doesn't take as long as I thought, and at the end, Tabby and I win by a landslide. Maybe because of our massive skills, but probably because no one besides Tabby really cares—except maybe Eleanor.

Troy is talking to her, smiling, resting his hand on her shoulder, but she's not looking at him. She's flushed in the face and glaring at Tabby.

Today is full of surprises.

The next event is a beanbag toss. The teams are each given their own uniquely colored beanbags and we have to get as many of our bags as we can into a bucket about thirty feet away—the same one we used for the water balloons. Each team gets a point for each bag.

The euphoria from winning the last event fades when I realize Tabby has the worst aim ever, and Eleanor has a great arm.

Troy and Eleanor handily win the event and Miss Viola announces there's a tie between two teams. The fourth and final round will determine the winner. Some of the competitors have meandered off, losing interest in the competitions, while others plop down with lunches to watch the end. It's down to two teams, me and Tabby versus Troy and Eleanor.

Miss Viola tells us each team has to pick one teammate to compete in the final game.

"What's the game?" I ask.

"Sumo wrestling."

As if it were preplanned, a door slides open from the back of the truck parked next to the field and two people jump out carrying giant, inflatable sumo suits.

"I'm not doing that."

Tabby has a feral grin on her face. "I'm so in."

They won't let Troy put on the sumo suit due to his size, so the final competition is between the two most competitive people on the field: Tabby and Eleanor. How appropriate.

They suit up. The sumo suits are giant, flesh-covered plastic suits stuffed with air and sporting fake G-strings.

It's going to take a while to push them in there, so I use the opportunity to sidle over to Miss Viola.

"Hey, Miss Viola." I stop next to her wheelchair.

"I'm not changing the scores."

I hold up my hands in surrender. "I'm not asking you to. I saw you talking to my aunt Leah."

"Oh, right. The charity lady. She mentioned her niece was competing. She seems nice. She was asking about the activities at the senior center. And about the library and if I knew anyone there."

Of course. They would be seeking intel on their main source of income. How else could they weasel their way into people's lives? But the library?

"Ruby!" Tabby yells at me.

Tabby and Eleanor have been poured into the suits and filled up. They both look ridiculous, but they don't seem to care.

Troy is with Eleanor on one side of the grassy field, evidently trying to pump her up for the final battle. Tabby is glaring daggers at the both of them.

"I need water," she tells me when I say goodbye to Miss Viola and make my way over to Tabby. I squirt some into her mouth from a water bottle we've got off to the side. It would feel like a real wrestling competition if it weren't for how silly the whole thing is.

"She's been favoring her left side," I tell Tabby.

"You think?"

"I know. Ever since the potato sack race, she's been rubbing her left thigh. Go there and she'll topple like a stack of bananas."

Miss Viola calls the opponents to the center of the field and explains that the last person standing is the winner. It doesn't matter whether they get knocked over by the opposing team or roll over on their own. I can see what she means since Tabby and Eleanor can barely stay upright, waddling around in the rounded, air-filled suits.

Miss Viola is back on the megaphone. "Three, two, one, go!" She shoots the gun into the air, grinning and whooping like Yosemite Sam.

The game is on.

At first, Tabby and Eleanor bob around each other, each of them looking like fat chickens that can't quite walk right. Then, unsurprisingly, Tabby goes for Eleanor's weak side.

"That's cheating!" Eleanor yells. "She's trying to kick me."

"I can't kick in this thing. I can barely move my leg." She demonstrates, kicking one leg up. It barely moves.

Eleanor grumbles but they get back into their bobbing stances.

"Go for her face!" Troy yells to Eleanor.

"Okay, that would definitely be cheating," Tabby says.

Troy shrugs. "You deserve it."

Eleanor lunges toward Tabby while she's distracted with Troy and bounces her stomach off of Tabby, sending Tabby over on one side.

"No!" she yells, reaching for Eleanor. She grabs her by the fabric of the suit and they both topple to the ground on their backs.

"I'm going to get you," Eleanor says, waving her arms and legs.

"Not if I get you first!" Tabby is in the same position. They both look like turtles who've fallen onto their shells, hands and feet waving uselessly in the air.

"Ruby, help me up!" Tabby yells.

I can't. I'm laughing so hard I can barely breathe. "You both look ridiculous," I say and then dissolve into laughter again.

"Well, who won?" Tabby asks.

"Neither of you won. You both went over at the same time," Miss Viola says.

"I demand a recount!" Tabby yells.

"There's nothing to count. You both win. I need a drink." She pushes a button on her wheelchair and drives it off toward the concession stands.

"Is someone going to help us get up?" Eleanor asks.

"I don't know, I kind of like you in this position." Troy considers her, rubbing his chin with one hand.

Tabby groans. "Oh, gross."

"If you don't help me up, when I do get up you will be sorry," Eleanor fumes.

"Yeah, same here. I will put itching powder in your jock when you least suspect it."

Eleanor laughs. "He would totally deserve it."

"Hey." Troy looks wounded. "Now I really don't want to help you." He crosses his arms over his chest.

"We don't need you anyway. Ruby!"

I take my time walking over, still chuckling as they wiggle around on the ground. It takes a few minutes, and Troy ends up helping Eleanor despite his words, and eventually we get them both back onto their feet and out of the suits.

"It was hot in those things." Tabby pulls on the front of her T-shirt. "I think we need a cold drink. Come on, ladies." She grabs my hand and then Eleanor's and drags us away from Troy.

"Hey, where are you guys going?"

"Don't worry about it, you big jerk," Tabby calls over her shoulder.

"Eleanor?"

Tabby keeps walking, still holding on to us both. "I'm going to tell them about the time I caught you wearing my dress."

"I was five!"

"It's still funny!"

Troy grumbles something behind us, but we keep walking.

Eleanor is not acting shy, not anymore. She's laughing and asking questions and as I watch them, a warm glow spreads through my chest.

Tabby will have a friend once I'm gone.

~*~

"There was a cat fight and I missed it?" Jared asks.

"It was more of a mouse fight."

Paige is dancing along about twenty feet in front of us while we walk back to Ruby's. How the girl still has so much energy is beyond me. My feet hurt.

After celebratory drinks with Tabby and Eleanor, Jared found us and stole me away. Then we in turn found Paige, who was playing carnival games with Greg and Gary. We sat in the grass in the late-afternoon sunshine and ate dinner from a food truck. Later, when the band started up, Jared and I danced under the stars.

I didn't see any sign of the parents. It was a good night.

Jared smirks. "I always miss all the fun."

"You didn't miss much. I'm glad Tabby and Eleanor are getting along now."

"Haven't they always gotten along?"

"I suppose so. I guess I'm just glad they're becoming better friends." And I really am. Tabby will need someone to talk to once I'm gone. But with the gladness comes a pang of something else. Guilt? To hide the emotion from my voice, I end the words on a big yawn.

"Well, I'm glad I'm bringing you home to tuck you into bed." Jared swings our linked hands up so he can kiss the back of my knuckles.

"It is a good thing." I smile up at him.

"What are you guys doing tomorrow night?"

"I'm not sure."

"Did you want to come over for dinner, with Paige?"

We haven't gone to Jared's since the parents made their appearance. I haven't exactly been avoiding it, but not going there has made it easier to believe that I've been protecting Jared somehow. But have I been, really? He's still here, with me. They still want me to use him for their own ends, and I still haven't figured out a way to stop them. Maybe I can go to his house and use it as a way to keep them at bay. Not by giving them what they want, but by appearing to do their bidding and buying me some time.

I shrug. "Sure."

"You have nothing planned? Are you sure?"

"Should I have something planned?"

"No," he says quickly, but I think he's hiding a smile. "You should invite your aunt and uncle, too. I really want to get to know your family more."

I swallow. "I'll check and see if they're free."

I'll do no such thing.

CHAPTER SEVEN

Everybody has had to deal with an uncomfortable family reunion.

Drunk uncles and fighting cousins. Shut-in aunts and busybody grandparents. Skeletons that trot out of the familial closet as soon as the eggnog starts flowing.

But when it comes to awkward-relative stories, I've got them all beat.

"You distract him and we'll search his office," Mother tells me as we're driving to Jared's for dinner.

I wish I could have prevented this. I didn't tell them about Jared's dinner invite. I had planned on making excuses for why they couldn't make it. But wouldn't you know it, they "happened" to run into him when he was taking his morning jog.

And since my car isn't working—or you know, I have no idea where it actually is or what they did with it—they so kindly offered to drive us over. And Jared, the bighearted sap, so kindly invited them to join us.

Giant eye roll.

Paige and I are in the back seat of the Mercedes, and even though the leather seats are plush and comfortable, we've both been squirming the entire ride.

Probably because as soon as we got in the car, the parents started grilling us for information on the layout of Jared's house, where he keeps his documents, likely places he would hide things of importance, all of that.

I had no choice but to tell them. After all, they'd given me quite a few days to get the information on my own and so far I'd failed.

When I started to make excuses—and it's true I haven't been to Jared's all week, because he's been coming over to our place—they shut me down. After all, if I had wanted an invite over to his house, they're sure I could have found a way.

I can't just blow them off anymore.

Then they told me what I would be expected to do. Mother will leave to powder her nose, and I will have to distract Jared so he doesn't notice if she's gone more than a couple of minutes. Well, dear Dad will be sure to help me, along with Paige.

Now I just need to figure out how to stop them. But do I want to stop them? Will they really sign over Paige if they get what they want? I'm not sure I can believe it. They aren't exactly paragons of integrity.

We pull into Jared's driveway and Father parks the car.

"You know the plan, right?" His eyes meet mine in the rearview mirror.

"Yes. Distract Jared, give you time to search. I get it. It's not rocket science."

"Watch your tone," Mother says.

I roll my eyes as I get out of the car.

We walk up the front porch together and I knock.

Jared answers after a few seconds, leaning in to kiss my cheek before he shakes hands with my Father and gives Paige a side hug.

"We brought some wine." Mother hands him a bottle with an expensive-looking label and kisses him on the cheek, leaving a deep red mark behind.

"Thanks. Come on in, I'll just put this bottle down." He leads us into the kitchen and then toward the living room.

"Why are all the lights off?" I ask. The sun is setting and the living room is gloomy. I'm not paying a ton of attention to the surroundings, though. I'm too busy trying to wipe the lipstick smudge from Jared's cheek. Her mark on him bothers me.

"I, uh, I'm not sure. You can turn the light in the living room on."

"Okay."

He's acting weird. I know something is up. A wayward idea shimmers in the back of my mind, something about today's date, so when a figure ducks behind the couch right before I click on the light, I'm not entirely surprised when—

"Surprise!"

The shouts explode while I'm still standing in the entrance to the living room. I don't have to fake my startled jump but I do lay it on a little thicker by shrieking and then laughing and cursing everyone. There's laughter and talking and a crowd swarming me for hugs.

It's not my birthday.

It's *Ruby's* birthday.

I wrote the date down on the tax forms I had to complete for the police station before I started consulting for them.

I'm still hugging people, but my mind is reeling a bit because Jared remembered. He noticed enough to throw me a party and plan something and get everyone out here.

I've never had a party before. No one has ever cared enough. Except Paige, but I could hardly expect my sister, who's eight years my junior, to plan me some kind of birthday party.

Immediately following the glow of surprise comes the ache of knowing it's all a farce. It's not really my birthday. It's yet another lie. And how do I repay him? By letting my parents into his home to scam him out of his money. Most people bring wine or gifts to the host. I bring destruction.

Did the parents know? When I glance around for them, they're shaking hands, meeting and greeting. Mother shoots me a look that says our plan will have to change.

They didn't know. If they had, they would have said something, found some way to weasel their way into being a part of it or using it somehow to their advantage.

There are quite a few people, more than I would have expected. There are the obvious: Jared, Tabby, Troy, and Eleanor. Ben. Mrs. Hale and Mrs. Olsen. Plus Mr. Bingel and the boys, Judge and Mrs. Ramsey, and even Miss Viola pretend-sleeping in her wheelchair—as usual. All of these people came here. For me?

"Why didn't you say anything about it being your birthday?" Tabby half hugs, half strangles me.

"I guess I just didn't think it was that big of a deal." I shrug it off.

"Not a big deal? My birthday is in a little over a week. We're practically twins!"

"Excuse me? Don't you mean triplets?" Troy interjects. "Happy birthday," he adds, giving me a quick hug and handing me a lumpy wrapped box with duct tape sticking off the sides. "It's not as good as a swap meet gift, but I think it's pretty good."

"Why is this wrapped in Christmas paper?"

He shrugs. "It's all I had."

"It's not time for presents, Troy," Tabby snaps.

"But I really want her to open it now."

"You're so annoying." Tabby's eyes roll heavenward and then she's distracted by conversation with Mrs. Ramsey.

Even though I'm probably too old to be excited about birthday presents, I can't help it. I want to open the gift now. It's hard to be a mature adult when I've never had anyone care enough to give me gifts and plan me parties. I rip open the Santa-covered wrapping paper. Inside the large box is a Ouija board and a Magic 8-Ball.

Troy grins at me. "In case you ever run out of tricks up your sleeve, you'll have a backup."

I swallow past a lump that's formed in my throat. I'm going to miss Troy. "That's so—"

"That's so sweet." Mother stands beside me and looks down at my present before turning her bright smile on Troy.

And the lump of emotion turns into a rock of frustration.

"You must be Officer Reynolds. I've heard so much about you." Mother takes his hand and shakes it, pulling him a little closer.

I plaster a smile on my face and then introduce them. "This is my aunt Leah."

"You can call me Troy."

"Troy." Her smile is dazzling. "It's such a strong name, and it suits you so well." She's still holding his hand, shaking it. Now she lifts one hand and clasps it around his bicep. "Does the department require you to stay so fit?"

Troy is immediately charmed, the grin on his face growing, though he tries to stay serious. "Well, you know, I've always felt it's important to stay in shape." He flexes an arm for her. "The public depends on me."

Mother nods and smiles at him just a beat too long, then clears her throat. "Oh, you must excuse me, the air here is so dry."

I have to refrain from rolling my eyes. It's not dry at all.

"I can get you some punch," Troy offers.

"Would you? You are such a sweet man."

He literally runs in the direction of the kitchen. How can he fall for such an obvious ploy?

As soon as he's gone, she leans over to whisper in my ear, a smile still plastered on her face. "Plan has changed. Father and I will search the study together."

It makes sense. With all of these people here, they won't need me to run a distraction. This crowd should be distracting enough. No one will notice if they disappear for a few minutes, and two people searching will move faster and more efficiently than one.

I nod, and then Troy is back with her drink. She turns away from me to take the glass from him and pepper him with more compliments.

"Can we go swimming?" Paige appears next to me. "The boys want to go in the pool." She gestures behind her to Greg and Gary, who are all puppy-dog eyes.

I glance around to find Jared and catch him watching us. He nods and makes a loud announcement to move the party outdoors, and then there's the hum of talking and laughing while everyone shifts the party outside.

I can't follow them yet, though. I don't know when the parents are going to make their move, but before long I know they will be digging through Jared's office.

I can't let them find anything.

While everyone is organizing food and games outside, I slip away, making an offhand comment to Tabby about using the restroom before slinking down the hall to Jared's office.

The computer is off, and bits of mail are strewn across the desk. I flip through them. Nothing looks important. I open a few drawers, finding some neatly sorted files. I shuffle through the documents, but there's nothing with account information on it. The folders labeled for taxes for the last three years are all empty. Where are they? I go through the rest of the drawers but I can't find anything else the parents could use against him. Maybe they won't have time to look any further than what I've done myself. They won't get into his computer—not easily and not without someone else's help. They've never been tech savvy.

There's a filing cabinet in the corner, but it's locked. I consider attempting to jimmy the lock with a paper clip, but then voices and laughter sound in the hallway.

No time for anything else.

I wait until the voices fade back down the hall and then I sneak out of the room, gently closing the door behind me.

By the time I reach the living room, everyone has made their way outside.

Most of the party is sitting or standing around a table that's been laid out with appetizers. The kids are in the pool. Troy is in there with them, tossing the boys around like they're rag dolls, making them shriek when they get splashed with the resulting spray.

The party is a blur of food, drinks, and laughter. If it were my actual birthday, it would be the best one ever. Except for the parents. But there are enough people here that I can almost forget about them. Until I'm talking to Judge Ramsey and Mother meets my eye from across the patio.

Her smile is just as friendly as the one she's used to charm everyone here, but I read the intent behind it.

Father reaches her side, and they both disappear into the house. No one appears to notice but me.

I try and focus on the party, on my conversation, but my heart thumps dully in my chest while I wait for them to reemerge.

No less than ten minutes later, they are back. They mingle and talk as normal, but there's a tightness in their eyes and a brittle undertone to their laugh.

Maybe they didn't find anything.

Then more food is brought out, and there's no time for me to discover whether they were successful or not.

After we eat, Tabby and Jared make me open presents. Mr. Bingel and the boys bought me a box of gardening supplies, the Ramseys got me a nice chess set, and Tabby got me a gift certificate for a spa day. Which I have to use with her and Eleanor, and Eleanor actually seems genuinely excited about the idea.

Off to one side, Mother explains to Mrs. Hale how they are planning on buying me a new car for my birthday. If I could roll my eyes without anyone seeing, I would.

The last gift is from Jared. The box isn't huge; it's square and rather flat and fits on my lap.

As unassuming as the package is, I'm stunned into silence when I get it open.

It's a signed and framed picture of Lucille Ball.

Paige lets out a low whistle. "Is that an original print?"

Of course, she would think the same thing that comes to my mind. What is this worth? Knowing Jared, probably a lot.

"That's an awesome gift," Tabby says. "You love Lucy."

"I do," I say, still a bit overwhelmed. "Thank you," I tell Jared. He's standing across the room so I can't kiss him, and I'm still not sure how I feel about public displays of affection with the parents watching, but hopefully he can see my thoughts in my eyes.

In fact, everyone must sense it because Troy says, "Someone's getting some tonight."

Eleanor hits him on the arm and Tabby rolls her eyes.

After presents, there's cake. Cheesecake. Of course, Jared remembered. "Even though it's not really cake," he adds with a wink.

By the time everyone leaves for the night, it's late.

"You're staying, right?" Jared asks as people are making their goodbyes in the entryway. "I can bring you home tomorrow."

"Paige can stay with us tonight," Father says.

I don't miss the flare of panic in Paige's eyes.

"She has an extra toothbrush and clothes here already," I say. "It would be easiest for her to stay. That way you don't have to drive all the way to our house for her stuff."

"That would be great," Jared interjects. "We could swim and I'll take you guys out to breakfast in the morning."

"Well isn't that nice." Mother smiles and weaves an arm through mine. "Will you walk me to the car, dear?"

"Of course."

As soon as we're in the driveway, she leans in and whispers, "We couldn't find any account statements. His files were all empty. Even the ones in the locked cabinet." She watches for my reaction and I have to use every acting ability I have to hide my relief at those words.

"That's too bad." So they were able to get into the cabinet. And it's empty, too. What the heck?

"That means you will need to hack into his computer. Do it tonight while he's sleeping." Without waiting for my response, she pulls me into a quick hug before sliding into the car.

Then Father is hugging me, too. It's all for show. "We'll come by tomorrow for the information. I'm sure you won't have any problems." He ruffles my hair like I'm a child he's fond of before he slides into the driver's seat.

Then they're pulling away and I'm left in the driveway staring after them.

I'm glad they couldn't find anything, but now how am I going to get around this? Tell them I couldn't find anything in the computer either? Will they believe me? Will they take Paige if I don't deliver?

Why are all of Jared's files missing anyway?

I can't leave him waiting too long. Back inside, Jared and Paige are in the kitchen cleaning up some of the leftover debris from the party. I help them. There's not much because people threw away all their stuff as they left. Within a few minutes we've got most of it put away except for a few dishes that Jared insists we leave in the sink.

Paige is yawning, so I send her to bed. She disappears into her old room, the one she used the last time we stayed with Jared.

"Thank you for today," I tell Jared when we're heading down the hall to his room. "The party, the presents, and everything."

He shrugs. "It's not much."

"It is, though."

He hands me a pair of his boxers and a T-shirt to wear to bed, and then we brush our teeth in the master bath at the double sinks. He's only wearing sleep pants, giving me a nice view of his chest and muscular arms. I smile around my toothbrush. We're the picture of domesticity.

But then I remember I have an ulterior plot to take care of. His computer was locked. It takes time to hack into a PC, time I might not have. There might be an easier way to get his password, although I'm loath to do it.

I finish brushing and wipe my mouth on a small towel before pretending to remember something. "Oh, hey, I almost forgot. Do you think I could use your computer real quick before bed? I was expecting something from a vendor yesterday, and it never showed up. I want to check my email since I haven't had a chance to check on the status."

He's nodding even before I finish my whole sentence. "Of course. You'll have to log in. The password is—"

I hold up a hand to stop him. He seriously can't make it this easy. I can't let him. "Why don't you just come type it in for me?"

What is he thinking? You can't just give your password out like that! I know I need it, but I don't *want* to need it. The warring emotions are tossing me about like a balloon in a tornado.

He quirks an eyebrow at me. "It's no big deal. My password is CastleCove911."

It hurts that he's trusting me when he shouldn't, but nonetheless his password makes me smile. I lean forward and kiss him softly on the lips.

"What was that for?"

"That was for being so cute." And trusting. The fool.

I leave him in his room and pad down the hall to the office, going inside and shutting the door partway before flicking on the lights.

Once behind the desk, I start up his computer and key in his password. My hands shake as I type the words. Why am I doing this?

It's for Paige, a small voice reminds me.

It doesn't make me feel any better.

Once I'm logged in, it doesn't take long to find what I'm looking for. Jared has his information saved, encrypted, in one of his drives. It's cute that he tried to store the information safely, but it's amateurish at best. It takes me mere minutes to unlock the files and then I have everything I need. Account numbers. Passcodes. Along with mutual funds, he also has various CDs and other investments that make up quite an impressive portfolio.

One account at a separate financial institution from the rest holds a paltry sum—for him. About fifteen thousand.

I don't print anything. Instead, I memorize as much of the information as I can. It's not hard to do, I've been trained for this. Some of the account numbers are long, but I mentally file them away by separating the long numbers into memorable chunks, an old tactic the parents taught me when I was younger than Paige.

When I'm done, I shut everything down and sit there for a minute, staring at the blank screen in front of me. Am I really going to do this?

"Hey," Jared calls from the doorway, wearing nothing but sleep pants and a smile.

"Hey."

"You ready?" He means for bed, and if the grin on his face is any indication, he doesn't mean for sleeping.

I'm not ready. Not ready for anything. But I nod.

CHAPTER EIGHT

The next day, I'm a ball of nerves and anxiety. I know they're going to show up asking for the intel at any moment.

Part of me wants them to, if only to catch the conversation on the recorder and cement my insurance policy.

But I still don't know if I'm going to give it to them. What will they do if I don't? If I refuse? Would they believe me if I told them I couldn't get it?

Of course, I *did* get it, or at least a little of it. The smaller bank account I found in Jared's name. Even acknowledging its existence inside my brain makes my head pound.

I could hack into it, transfer the money, and use it to run.

I could get Paige out of here. Jared wouldn't miss the money. Hell, he already offered it to her for college. And I seriously doubt she'll be going to college if I don't get her away from the parents. So it would be just like . . . borrowing against her college fund.

When I close up the shop for a few minutes during lunch, I go so far as to log into his account on the computer upstairs.

I stare at the account, mouse hovering over the balance.

After five minutes of trying to force myself to click, I log out and close the browser.

I can't do it.

I tell myself it's because if we run now, the parents will just find us again. They'll be on our tail forever. Better to face them now and find a way to keep Paige safe from them for good.

That's definitely a part of it, but another big part is Jared. And this town. I can't do it to him. I can't leave my parents here to finish whatever scam they're running on the people here.

It's not right.

I will do whatever it takes to stop them. I have to.

Decision made, I head back downstairs to open the shop again. Every time the bell over the shop door rings, my stomach drops into my toes, anticipating their arrival. By the time I'm ready to close up the shop, they still haven't showed. I'm not sure if I should be relieved or freaked out even more.

The phone rings and I nearly jump out of my skin.

"Ruby's Readings and Cosmic Shop," I answer, slightly breathless.

The voice on the other end is bossy and irritated. "We're going to Ben's." It's Tabby.

My anxiety settles down to a low simmer. She keeps talking before I can respond.

"And when I say 'we,' I mean me and you. And Eleanor. She has to work late, but she's meeting us there later."

"What's going on at Ben's?"

"Oh you know. People, music, the Newsomes fighting, maybe some pool playing and general shenanigans."

"Okay." Jared's on duty tonight anyway so I'll only see him if he gets called to the bar for work purposes.

I wonder if I could rile up the Newsomes myself, if only to see Jared for a brief moment.

When he's there, it's like everything else ceases to exist.

And maybe if I'm not home tonight, I can avoid the parents for another day.

"What time are we going?"

~*~

Ben's is surprisingly busy for a Monday night. Then again, most of the population is retired, so it's not like they have work in the morning.

Even more surprising, Ben doesn't yell at Tabby when she goes around the bar to get us some drinks. He just kisses her on the cheek and lets her do whatever she wants.

"What's up with that?" I ask when she brings our drinks back to our table, a pitcher of beer and three cups. One is for Eleanor, who hasn't yet arrived.

"What's up with what?"

"Ben didn't yell at you."

"Oh, yeah. He's still groveling. He's so my bitch right now. You need anything done around your house?"

"Not at the moment."

"Seriously, I can hook you up. You need your lawn mowed, heavy things lifted, or a toilet unclogged, I got a guy for at least another month."

"Well, I'm glad he's taking the time to suck it up."

She smiles. "Me, too. After your birthday party, we went up to the point and made out like teenagers."

I laugh.

"Until the Newsomes showed up." She frowns. "They always ruin everything. Sheila was moaning and screaming so loud, she sounded like Mr. Newsome was trying to kill her. It was so not sexy."

I grimace. "I've seen and heard all of that before. I don't need a reminder."

"Sorry I'm late." Eleanor slides into the booth next to Tabby. "We have an event coming up at the library, a fundraiser, so we're making a bunch of plans. It ran longer than I expected."

My ears perk up at the word fundraiser. Is that why mother asked Miss Viola about the library?

"What kind of fundraiser?" I ask as Tabby pours Eleanor a drink from the pitcher and slides it over.

"Oh, just a new thing we're doing for literacy in third-world countries. With your aunt and uncle, actually." She brightens. "We started talking at your birthday party and they're going to help us with the event."

And my night takes a nosedive.

"Did I miss anything interesting?" Eleanor changes the subject. I'm both grateful and annoyed. What else are they planning?

"Nope," says Tabby. "I was just telling Ruby how I ran into the Newsomes out at the make-out spot."

"Ugh." Eleanor takes a small sip of her beer. "I found them one time at the library. Back in the rare fiction section."

Tabby gasps. "No!"

"Yes. People hardly ever go back there, it's true, but still. They were not reading and they were not using library voices."

Tabby snorts. "What did you do?"

"What could I do? I ran away. When they checked out their books, I could hardly look at them. Especially when I saw what they were reading."

"You have to tell us what it was."

"There was one about tantric sex, a couple on the Kama Sutra."

I force myself to laugh along with Tabby, though I must not be doing a good job of it because Tabby gives me a look. I'm too trapped in my own head, thinking about the parents.

"How clichéd," I add weakly.

"But the other was a book on how to teach physics to your dog."

"Do they even have a dog?" Tabby wrinkles her nose in confusion.

I was in Mrs. Newsome's house after they had a break-in. I don't recall dogs, dog hair, or any other indication there were any kind of pets around. Only Mr. Newsome, and maybe some sex toys. "I don't think so. But they've found a way to keep their passion alive. I think it's kind of sweet.

Tabby snorts out a laugh. "You're drunk."

"I've only had a few sips."

"You're hallucinating. Maybe psychotic. There's nothing cute or sweet about the Newsomes."

"It's sweet how into each other they still are, after so many years."

"They're divorced."

"Yeah, but it works for them. We should be so lucky to be as into our significant others as they are when we're their age."

"That might be true. Do you think you'll still want to jump Jared's bones when you're sixty?"

I shrug, uncomfortable with the question. I'm not going to know Jared when I'm sixty, so this conversation is moot.

"I think Troy and I—"

Tabby points at her. "Not you, blondie. I don't want to hear shit about you and my brother. You are cut off from this conversation."

"Oh, come on, Tabby. Eleanor can talk about Troy. Maybe just keep any talk of Newsome-like activity to a minimum."

"Minimum? Try not any." Tabby shudders.

Eleanor just laughs. "Well, he is taking me to the fundraiser. We decided to have a gala."

"A gala?" Tabby asks. "Sounds fancy."

"It will be pretty fun. David and Leah are talking about having a silent auction for businesses to donate services and goods, plus dancing and a charity dinner."

"What an awesome idea. They are so cool," Tabby says.

"Yeah." I nod. "They're so great."

Tabby refills my beer glass. I didn't even realize I'd drunk the whole thing.

They continue to talk, the conversation fluttering around me, Tabby and Eleanor discussing the charity, the gala, what they're going to wear, and how Tabby can help with the event. Then they move on to Troy and Tabby's birthday party—some kind of bonfire on the beach. A tradition they've kept up every year since they were teenagers. It's on a Tuesday this year, which is weird, but they never break the tradition—always on their birthday no matter which day of the week it falls.

My stomach settles down when the conversation turns to other things and there's no more mention of the parents or anything to do with them.

But then Eleanor is waving and smiling at someone across the room.

The parents. And they're heading this way.

"I told them I was going to Ben's; they must have come to check it out," Eleanor tells us. Then she's sliding out of the booth to stand and greet them. "Hey, it's nice to see you again so soon."

I focus on the glass in my hands.

I can't look. My face is frozen in a smile. They're going to ask if I got the information. I thought maybe I had avoided them for the day, but of course, they tracked me down.

Tabby shifts next to me, and then she's standing and hugging them. "It's so nice to see you," she says.

I have to act normal. I have to act like they're my beloved aunt and uncle.

I can do this. For Paige.

"Hey, guys." I stand up and fix a bright smile on my face.

As expected, my "aunt" and "uncle" each give me big hugs, and Mother even kisses me lightly on the cheek. I resist the urge to rub it off.

Of course Tabby and Eleanor invite them to join us and we all sit around the booth. I manage to nab a seat on the end so I have an easy escape route.

"It's so nice to hang out with some of Ruby's family," Eleanor says.

"Our nieces mean so much to us," Mother says. "We never were able to have children of our own." She touches the string of pearls around her neck, her eyes going misty.

Eleanor makes a sympathetic sound. "That's so sad."

I cough.

"That's why we got involved in charity work, like with the library. It feels really good to give back to people, especially children."

I have to tune them out before my internal screaming escapes. They talk to my friends, all smiles and happy exuberance. They talk about the charity and some other work they've done—all lies—but it's so convincing. A mass of anxiety and anger slushes around inside me, building up and up. I can't sit here and listen to this.

I know I'm being a hypocrite. I'm conning my friends. I have been this whole time, but it's different somehow.

"I have to use the restroom." I think I interrupt someone midsentence, but it can't be helped.

I slide out of the booth and rush to the bathroom like I might explode—which I might, but not in the way one usually does when racing for a toilet. I don't see their faces or their response to my sudden departure. All I see is red. The restrooms are down a long hallway at the back of the building, where it's thankfully quieter and less crowded.

Once in the bathroom, I sequester myself in a stall and force myself to calm down. I knew this was coming. They weren't going to leave me alone forever. But now they're here and talking to my friends—*conning* my friends—and I'm going to have to deal with it. Panic will not help me, or them. Or Paige.

I force myself to breathe for a few minutes and then exit the stall. The person staring back at me from the other side of the mirror doesn't look as crazy as I feel, so I have that going for me. I splash some water on my face, hoping the parents will have left the building by now, or at least not be talking to my friends anymore.

All my hopes are dashed as soon as I open the door.

They're waiting for me.

Mother throws down the gauntlet. "You have some information to share with us."

CHAPTER NINE

"Well, where is it?" Father asks. The toothpick in the corner of his mouth jumps with his words.

Gone are the placating smiles and soft voices.

I've ushered them even farther down the long hallway, near a rear exit and away from the bathroom doors. Can't risk being overheard by anyone.

"I don't have anything."

"Lies," Mother hisses. "You were there all night and this morning. You had plenty of opportunity."

"I tried. I was in his office and he interrupted me before I could get what you want. He's going to get suspicious. I just need more time."

"We don't have all the time in the world," Father says. "Eventually, Ruby will be returning. If she comes back before we get what's ours, you'll be going down. And what do you think will happen to your sister then?"

"We still have almost a month. Give me a couple weeks."

I know they'll never agree, but I have to aim high to get them to settle for something in the middle. I just need more time to figure out what to do, which means stalling them.

"No," Father says. "That's way too long."

"Why do you need Jared's information right now? You're already running a scam with this whole charity thing. And I thought you weren't skimming his funds until after the charity con had run its course. How many times have you said that doubling a con gets you triple the time?"

"The charity thing is child's play," Mother says with a wave of her hand. "Barely enough to live on. We have no choice. We need money to eat, don't we? Since we obviously can't count on *you* to help us." Her voice brims with harsh disapproval.

We stand in the hall in silence. I'm not sure what to say. I can't give them what they want, even though I have it. Hell, I couldn't even use it for myself. How can I hand it over to *them*?

"We'll give you two days."

I have to work to mask my surprise. That was easy. Too easy. They never capitulate that quickly.

Father makes a disgusted sound, like he wants to argue, but Mother puts a hand on his arm and continues. "If you don't get the account information, we'll expose you and take Paige. This is your last chance."

And with that, they head back down the hall and into the bar to schmooze more with my friends.

I stand there, in the shadowed corner, thinking.

At least I have two more days. That was the only good thing to come out of our conversation.

But why? She gave in way easier than I thought she would. There's no reason they couldn't just take Paige now and run. Why didn't they already? The only explanation is they need this money. Badly. And for that, they need me. Maybe I have more leverage than I realized.

Another thought filters through my head, making more and more sense the more I think on it. They've got to be planning something else. They wouldn't just ask about some account numbers and then let me and Paige go—this whole thing is too easy.

There's more up their sleeves than what they're showing.

There always is. Maybe I can find out what it is and turn this blackmail around on them.

But how can I find out what they're truly after and why?

~*~

"We should spy on them," Paige says. "Even when we lived with them, it wasn't too difficult. I tailed them all the time."

The morning after the parents' surprise visit at Ben's, Paige and I are in the kitchen eating breakfast and discussing our ruination. I don't want to worry her or involve her at all, but she's the only one I can talk to about everything.

And she makes a good point. Since the passive surveillance efforts aren't working, it's time to up my game. Of course, they'll be on their guard this time.

"I can follow them," Paige offers when I don't respond quickly enough.

I choke on my juice. "No way. Too dangerous." If they catch her on their tail, they'll grab her—and there's no way in hell I'll be able to talk them into giving her back a second time.

She rolls her eyes and sticks a forkful of waffle in her mouth.

Once upon a time, when they weren't rushing a double con and blackmailing their daughter into helping, they had a brush with the FBI. For a while, they got fanatical about security, only discussing jobs outdoors, in crowded or noisy places impossible to bug. When they found out they were on the FBI's watch list, they were both annoyed and flattered to be under such scrutiny. Of course, that was a while ago and I think the feds have lost interest since. Bigger fish to fry and not enough in the budget. But still, the parents developed a few paranoid habits Paige used to take advantage of.

Every night, they would disappear for a few hours and take a walk. Then they'd discuss all the details for a job they hadn't wanted Paige and me to know about. Or they'd meet co-conspirators or their fence to exchange goods. They made it quite the habit, actually. Do they still? Humans are creatures of habits, even con artists whose job it is to understand and take advantage of said habits. They're not afraid of bugged buildings anymore if they're blabbing at Ruby's. But maybe they're still night owls.

"You're right," I say. "I'll just have to follow them at night."

"How are you going to manage that without them knowing? You're not the one with experience tailing them."

If this were a cartoon, a light would click on over my head. "I need a tracker."

Paige's eyebrows lift. "How are you going to find something like that? We only have the cameras, and they're not GPS enabled."

It means more deception, more of using Jared to achieve my own ends, but . . . is there any other choice? "I have an idea." And I only have two days to do it.

CHAPTER TEN

Stealing from the police station is easier than I anticipated.

The parents are right. People here are way too trusting.

Everyone knows I'm Jared's girlfriend, so Maggie, who works the dispatch counter, lets me pass right on through. I use the excuse of bringing Jared lunch—which is true. I even brought her a coffee with extra sugar, just like she likes it, which is a totally wasted effort because she needs no additional bribe.

Jared and I eat burgers from Stella's in his office, but we've barely finished eating when he has to get back to work.

"I'll walk you out." He stands but I put a hand on his chest and kiss him.

"I can find the way, you have enough to do."

He attempts to protest, but I kiss him again, and again until he stops and forgets what he's doing—until I nearly forget what I'm doing.

Once we're both a bit breathless, I'm free to exit the building on my own, although I have to stop for a minute outside Jared's door to collect myself.

I know exactly where to go. Instead of heading out the front door, I slip down the hall that leads to the archives and make my way down the deserted stairs. I've been down there before, when Jared and I were searching for information about the Knights and Ladies of the Red Baron, the old Castle Cove secret society that was the impetus behind the Castle Cove Bandit.

I find the locked cage readily enough, right next to some lockers labeled *Evidence Storage*.

It doesn't take much to jimmy the simple lock and locate the trackers, stuffed in between a new camera with night-vision lenses and a recording device that looks like a simple pair of glasses. There's also the magnet, wrapped in foam.

I bite my lip, considering it for a moment, and then I shove the magnet into my purse with the trackers.

You never know.

I haul ass back up the stairs on the balls of my feet, stopping first outside the door and listening to make sure no one is walking by. Then I'm out the door, shutting it softly behind me and walking down the hall like I didn't just steal sensitive police equipment.

Now that that's done, I need an innocuous vehicle. I stop by the hardware store on my way back to Ruby's.

"Can I borrow your car?"

Tabby isn't busy. There are no customers in the store. She's sitting at the front counter with her feet up, thumbing through a magazine. Maybe I should have prefaced the question with light conversation and chitchat, but there's really no time for any dancing around the topic.

"Sure," Tabby says without even blinking. "You want the keys now?"

"If that's okay."

She twists around, pulls the keys from a rack behind the counter, and tosses them to me, then goes back to her magazine.

"You're not going to ask why I need it?" I had a whole story planned about taking Paige on an overnight trip to Portland for bra shopping.

She shrugs. "I figure you'll let me know later if I need to help you bury a body."

"You're a good friend, Tabby." The words shoot an arrow straight through my chest. I don't deserve her trust.

"Don't you forget it." She points at me and turns back to her magazine.

I leave Tabby's car a couple of streets away from Ruby's and walk the rest of the way.

Now, I just have to wait.

Jared is working over the next few nights. Part of me misses him and wishes I could spend more time with him, but it works out because I'm free to spy.

Once the sun sets and Paige is asleep and safely locked in the house, I head out the door to Tabby's car. Her inconspicuous, midsized, older-but-not-too-old sedan is perfect for espionage. It's basically the same car almost everyone in town has. Totally an old lady car.

When I drive by the parents' house, a few lights are on and the Mercedes is parked in the driveway.

The house itself isn't as ostentatious as they would normally choose, but Castle Cove isn't exactly a mecca for the rich and wanna-be famous. It's still nice, though, sheened in upper-middle-class elegance. It has two stories, a wraparound porch, bay windows out front, and dormer windows up top. It's an elegant piece of real estate and I can't help but wonder how much they're paying for it. How much the citizens of Castle Cove are going to be paying for it.

After my drive-by, I park down the street and wait.

Once I plant the tracker on them, the plan is to show up at their house tomorrow. Surprise them, so to speak, so that by tomorrow night they'll have something they need to talk about.

I sit there in the dark, watching, until the lights go off around midnight.

Then I creep out of the car and plant the tracker under the rear bumper, pushing it back as far as I can before activating the sensor. I run back to Tabby's car and click the button on my end of the tracker's receiver, synching the items up so I'll be notified once they're on the move.

The light on the little handheld device clicks on, a glowing green dot where they're parked.

"Gotcha," I whisper.

Lights in the rearview mirror blind me momentarily. I sink down in the seat as an innocuous sedan cruises by. It looks rather like the car I'm in, actually.

Weird.

The taillights disappear around the corner.

A loud rapping on the passenger side startles a shriek from my throat.

A light shines into the window, pointing just beside my face to avoid blinding me.

"What are you doing?"

Oh, shit.

It's Jared.

CHAPTER ELEVEN

"Are you okay?" Jared asks when I don't answer his question.

"I'm good. I was just, uh, I came over here to have dinner with Dave and Leah." I cup my hand over the tracker. It's not very large, but it's also not completely covered by my hand. Dear god, don't let him shine his light in my lap.

"It's after midnight."

"Oh my gosh, is it? I had a glass of wine with dinner and I was just out here . . . thinking and I must have fallen asleep." I rub my eyes with one hand, the one not covering the tracker, to avoid meeting his gaze.

"Is your car not running again? Didn't you guys just get a new one? Do you want me to take a look at it tomorrow?"

I swallow. I'm in Tabby's car. Of course, he would offer to fix my car instead of wondering what the hell I'm doing and why. Why does he trust me so much?

"Yeah, well, it's already in the shop so Tabby let me borrow her car."

He leans down, inches from my face, his eyes serious, and I'm pretty sure he's going to call me out on my crappy lies. "I'm glad you're here."

"You are?" *Because you're going to arrest me now?*

"I've always wanted to make out in the back of the cruiser."

A bark of laughter escapes me, releasing some of my nerves. "I'll meet you there in two minutes."

As soon as he walks away, I let out a sigh of relief and hide the tracker under the seat.

Thirty minutes later, we've steamed up the windows in the police cruiser and he's handing me back my shirt. "Is this new?"

"No." It's just a plain, black T-shirt. I haven't worn it until now because it's too hot in June to be wearing black during the day.

He then hands me my pants, which are also black.

"Are you sure you weren't out here going to a funeral?" he teases, his voice light.

I laugh. "I guess I got dressed tonight without really looking at what I was putting on."

"Did you have a nice dinner with David and Leah?"

I don't answer for a moment, pulling my shirt over my head. "Yeah, it was good."

"Paige didn't want to come?" He's buttoning up his uniform. He didn't have to take off as much as I did.

"No, she, uh, wanted to chill at home."

"That doesn't really seem like her."

"Oh, well, you know. Teenagers." I roll my eyes. "She's getting to that age."

"I guess. I better get back to work." He's finished getting his uniform buttoned up and he leans over to kiss me on the lips.

It's not until I'm back in Tabby's car and driving home that I wonder what he was doing in their neighborhood. It's not normally where he patrols, since it's a residential area. Unless he was out on a call . . . I shake my head to clear away the thought. I'm seeing conspiracies everywhere.

~*~

The next morning, I wake up bright and early and head back to the parents' house.

Time to go Chuck Norris on their asses.

It's still early in the morning when I knock on their door. Now I'm the one coming after them. Part of my plan involves the element of surprise. I've never stood up to them before, ever. I've never been one to talk back to them or even suggest anything. They've always had me in my place. Well, no longer.

I alternate knocking and ringing the bell for about five minutes until the door finally opens.

"Good morning," I say brightly.

Mother is in a robe and slippers, her hair tied up in a messy knot and a sleeping mask pushed up on her forehead.

They never were morning people.

"What are you doing here?"

"Today's my deadline. Remember?" I walk past her into the house.

"And you're so anxious to turn over lover boy's money that you had to show up first thing?" Father asks from the staircase. He's also in a robe, just from bed, his hair a scruffy mess.

It's odd to see them this way, not all put together and perfect—sort of vulnerable. It almost makes them look human.

The inside of the house is as nice as it looks on the outside. Furnished, but entirely too homey for them. Overstuffed couches in the living room. Flowers on the dining table. The walls are painted a cheery, pale yellow.

"Actually no. I'm here to offer you a deal."

Father's face flushes. "We don't want a deal. We told you what we want."

"If you leave town today, I'll give you ten thousand dollars, plus another two thousand a month for the next five years." It's all bluster. I know they won't take it, but I need to figure out what they *will* take and stall them with it.

Mother laughs. "Do we look like a bank? Your offer is ridiculous and you know it. We want a payout now. We're not going to wait any longer."

And there it is, confirmation that they can't wait any longer. Hence the rushing and the pushing. What do they really want? Jared's money? Is that my only leverage?

Time to test my theory.

"I get it. But no matter what you want, there's not enough time to run a real con here. Ruby will be back and we'll have to be gone before then. We need to start over somewhere else. Paige and I will go with you and pay you back and do what you want to get your money."

As if. *Come on, come on, call my bluff.*

"No, no, no." Mother shakes her head. "No new deals. We know what we want, and you're going to give it to us one way or another."

"Fine. But I still need more time."

"You're stalling us on purpose. I bet you have those numbers already."

Of course I am. But it's what they'd expect from me at this point—I've done a lousy job of hiding my feelings for Jared. I stay silent for a moment, letting the conversation cool. "I don't know how you expect me to hand over something I don't have."

"I don't know how you expect us to not take Paige and turn you in. We've been lenient up till now. But you're forcing us to act."

Annnd time to dangle the bait. "Fine. I have one account number."

The small one not connected to the others. They'll need more, but this little taste will give them incentive to wait while I follow them around, unravel their true scheme, and prepare an escape hatch for Paige.

"Come on." Mother stands and motions me to follow her up the stairs. "We'll check it out now before you leave to make sure it's not a trick."

"I know better than to trick you."

"I would hope so, by now."

Father stays downstairs while I follow Mother up. She leads me down a hall and into an office.

"Here." She points at the computer—a top-of-the-line model—resting on the large oak desk. "Show me the account details."

"I'm not going to transfer any funds from here."

"I know. I just want to see it. We have a guy for the transfers."

A guy who can probably make the transfer untraceable, at least for as long as it takes for them to get what they need and disappear.

It takes a few minutes to pull up the account and while I'm tapping away, I glance around surreptitiously. Is there anything to give away their plans? Of course not. They wouldn't leave anything lying around.

Father calls out something from downstairs and Mother sighs.

"Don't touch anything." As she's leaving, she stops and bends over by the door, grabbing the document safe, the same one they've been carting around my whole life, and leaves with it.

Why did she do that?

She had to realize removing the safe from the room does nothing but bring it to my attention.

Is it a ruse? They want me to think something important is in the safe?

Or maybe something important is actually in there.

I glance around the office again, looking for any clues. But there's nothing out of place. Except for one of Father's mint toothpicks on the corner of the desk.

Which might come in handy for what I have planned.

I grab a tissue from a box on the table and pick up the toothpick, shoving it into my bra.

Then I get back to the computer, pulling up the information as quickly as I can, before Mother returns.

I've almost reached the right screen when she appears in the doorway.

"Do you have it yet?" She's still in her robe, but the sleeping mask is gone and her hair is pulled back into a neater bun.

"Um, yeah." I tap a few more keys and pull up the screen right as she comes around the desk.

There's a silence so loud it nearly hums as she reads over the information.

"There's only fifteen thousand in this account."

I clear my throat. "I guess so."

"This isn't nearly enough. We can't do anything with chump change."

"Well it's all I have. I can get the other account numbers. I just need more time."

"Your father isn't going to like this." Her lips press together.

I shrug, turning back to the computer to close out the screens. "I can't do anything about that."

She's quiet for so long I finally turn around and look up at her.

Her eyes meet mine, and something in them softens. "Charlotte, I—"

"Leah!" Father yells from downstairs again. Her fake name, not her real one.

It's just as well. Whatever she was going to say was probably a load of crap anyway. Something to butter me up, manipulate me somehow. It's what they do.

I try not to let it bother me. It's not me, it's them. I know that.

But it still hurts.

She's my mother.

I stand up. "I better go. I'll have to get more information from Jared to keep you guys happy." The sarcasm leeches into my tone.

She sighs and shuts her eyes, shaking her head. "I'll talk to your Father. I might be able to get you a few more days. You need to hurry. If we run out of time, you'll lose everything."

I nod, watching her closely. More manipulation? Probably. She's the good cop now.

I leave their house minutes later, feeling a little wobbly but more energized than I have since they showed up. Now to find out what they're really planning.

~*~

The same night, I park a few blocks away on a cul-de-sac that gets even less traffic than the parents' street. Maybe this way I can avoid getting caught again by Jared.

It's only a matter of time. At about ten o'clock, the Mercedes pulls out of the garage like a sleek and silent shark.

They aren't easy to tail, so having the tracker is invaluable. I follow the little dot on the screen, staying far enough behind them that they won't even see the lights from Tabby's car. They follow a familiar road and I know their destination before we're even halfway there. They're heading to Castle Cove Park. When the dot stops, I park the car and get out, pulling on a black beanie to cover my hair.

They've picked a great place to hide their conversation; it's too windy to hear much without getting close enough to be spotted. But I have to try.

They've left the car in the parking lot next to the little playground. Thankfully, there are trees and bushes I can hide behind and peer around while I stalk their location. They're at the top of the hill, their backs facing me as they stand side by side.

The wind is blowing in from over the sea and I slink behind them, sticking to the shadows around the trees surrounding the open grassy area. I'm glad I wore all black again; it helps me blend into the shadows.

This might actually work in my favor since the wind throws their words in my direction. Even so, I can only hear bits and pieces.

"She's not going to . . . account . . . information," Father says.

"She will if we . . . Paige."

"I don't know. She's changed. She loves him."

My mouth drops open and I want to protest. I do not love him. I like him. A lot. I greatly admire him. I . . . esteem him. I don't know, maybe I love him. Dammit.

Mother laughs, the sound full of derision. "She's an idiot."

She's not wrong.

Long seconds pass while they keep talking but I can't hear any of it.

Then— "It won't . . . account number or not. We'll get it ourselves eventually. Especially after we turn her in. You can be the one to help the grieving deputy through this trying time."

"What if she does . . . ? We need money . . ."

Father shrugs. "We'll turn her in anyway . . . and Paige. Can't . . . without her. No one can find out about . . ."

My blood runs colder than the wind over the sea. What do they need Paige for? What can no one find out about?

"Wait and see . . . either way, we'll get what we want. No one will suspect—"

Their voices jump in volume as they turn and head in my direction. I duck back into the shadows and slide myself around the boulder, keeping out of their line of sight as they move back toward the car.

They drive away while I stay huddled behind the boulder.

They're going to turn me in anyway? Even if I give them what they want?

Then what's the point? Why bother with all of these shenanigans? Why didn't they just take Paige when they had the chance and run?

They need money, and they need me. For what yet, I'm not sure, but there's got to be a good reason they didn't just take Paige and run that first night.

What do they want from me?

I need to cast suspicion on them. Turn the tables in my favor. Instead of being the one on the run, I want to send them scampering. I need to find a way to expose them for who they really are without getting caught in the crossfire.

And I have an idea.

I'm going to frame them. Not with something as inglorious as the truth, but by setting them up for a fall.

I step out from behind the boulder and run right into a warm body.

CHAPTER TWELVE

"Doug, is that you?"

What. The. Crap. It's Mrs. Newsome. She's barely dressed, wearing a nightie that is nothing but a silk scrap of fabric trimmed with black lace.

She's also blindfolded.

Small mercies.

I scamper away from her as silently as I can, back behind the boulder, my eyes darting around the park, looking for Mr. Newsome.

My guess is he's not blindfolded.

What is this, some kind of kinky hide-and-go-seek?

"Sheila, you're supposed to call me Captain!" Doug hisses.

His voice sounds from somewhere beyond Mrs. Newsome. Relieved, I scoot farther away. In the woods to the left, a bush jiggles.

"I just ran into someone," Sheila yells. "I have to take off my blindfold."

"No, just leave it on. There's no one out here but us."

"What if it's a murderer?"

"There's no murderer." He pauses. "Unless you want to pretend there is?"

"No . . . Maybe it's some pervert trying to catch us on film."

There's a pause while Doug seems to consider it. "That could be true."

I cover my mouth with my hand to stop the laughter from erupting.

"Come over here. Let's just do the final scene and go home."

"But the best part is when you fight the sheriff over Francesca's hand," Mrs. Newsome complains.

She stumbles toward him. Which means her back is to me and the rest of the park.

I flit from the boulder to a nearby tree, trying to stay out of view. It helps that they're so freaking loud.

The bushes rustle and a loud moan emanates from the woods where I last heard Mr. Newsome.

The sound makes me move faster—but I still keep to the shadows.

"Did you see that?" Sheila hisses.

Dammit.

"No, don't stop doing that with your tongue," Mr. Newsome complains.

"I just saw someone. They're in all black. It looked like a ninja or something."

Mr. Newsome sighs and grumbles. "There's no one there, Sheila."

"I know what I saw!"

Silence. And then, "Does it make it more exciting if you think there's someone watching us?" His voice is drowsy with lust.

Mrs. Newsome giggles. "Maybe."

I cringe into the darkness.

Not wanting them to see me, I force myself to wait, wanting to plug my ears but I can't until they're . . . suitably distracted. Then I sprint away, circling around the park and back to the main road. Out of sight—and hearing—distance.

Back in Tabby's car, I can't help but laugh.

And then I remember the parents' conversation and the laughter dries up.

Keep Paige safe.

I need to get home and set the wheels in motion.

~*~

The sun is descending into the ocean and the last of the beachgoers are packing up their things as I walk along the water, sandals in one hand and a world of trouble in the other.

Problem one. What do they really want with Paige? Based on what I overheard, they can't do *something* without her. But what could they possibly need her for? She's a thirteen-year-old girl for crying out loud.

My blood runs as cold as the Pacific water rushing between my toes.

There's really only one thing they could need her for that badly. Before we bailed on the parents, I was working as a maid in this old millionaire's house, casing the joint for antiquities to steal. But it wasn't enough for the parents. They wanted me to seduce Wallace. When I refused, Mother made a comment about Paige.

I'm sure we could find a use for your sister.

I'd assumed they meant for the things they used to make me do. Petty theft, obtaining intel.

But then there had been that guy, that big-shot attorney the parents had entertained not too long ago. They'd made Paige serve the drinks the night he came over for dinner, which wasn't normal procedure. If anything, they usually kept Paige away from people, out of school, only using her for cons where she could sneak around and not be seen. Had they wanted him to see Paige?

The thought makes bile churn in the back of my throat.

If that's the case, they are in worse than I thought, going through the hassle of coming here to blackmail me.

What if this guy wants Paige, and they intend to give her to him?

But if that's why they're here, why didn't they just take her and be done with it? They had her the night we tried to escape. Why not take her then?

Maybe this con is so they don't have to hand her over. She's always been their favorite. They aren't exactly models of parenting, but they've always treated her better than they've treated me. In some way, shape or form, do they care about her enough to try and protect her from this? By having me run this con?

It makes a sick sort of sense.

Why else give in to my demands? Simply to keep me under their thumb until they can find a way to set me up and take the fall for things they've done?

And why is Mother seemingly helping me? She's the reason I have a few more days. Is it part of their plan? Do they also need a few days to set up a frame against me? And the way she called attention to the safe . . . it might be a trap, but I can't help but be curious. What do they keep in there?

What I need is to cast suspicion on them. Once the local authorities have a reason to investigate, they'll start digging for sure, egged on with help from the local psychic. It shouldn't take much for the parents to fall.

It's not hard to plan a robbery. Except for the part where I have to be the thief and connect the crime to the parents instead of myself.

I consider staging a theft at Ruby's. I could plant the items in their car or house. I could use my "psychic" abilities to inform the cops and point the finger at them. But that's not enough. And I can't risk them turning the tables on me. I can't let the crime lead anywhere close to me.

I'm almost to the boardwalk. I stop on the beach, my toes sinking in the soft, wet sand, and gaze up at the shops.

There's Tabby's store. I wince; so not happening. There's a candy shop, the Castle Cove Restaurant, some touristy stores with hats and T-shirts. All small potatoes. On Main Street, there's the post office, a barbershop, a used bookstore, and . . . a jewelry store.

Bingo.

~*~

The owner of the jewelry store is a petite woman in her late sixties named Pearl. Her hair is gray but styled in a youthful bob. She's wearing a button-up blouse with slacks. She's dressed rather like Eleanor, so I'm not surprised when she tells me she's heard all about me.

"My niece Eleanor told me you're a friend of hers." Pearl bobs her head in my direction. Her voice is higher pitched than I expected at first glance, almost childlike.

"Yes. We've met. She's very kind."

The store itself is narrow and dim, most of the illumination coming from the glass cases, where inset lights set off gleaming rows of jewelry and baubles. It makes it harder to see at a glance if there's any type of surveillance on the ceiling.

"Are you looking for something in particular?" Pearl asks.

"I'm just window-shopping." I smile. "I can't afford anything like this, but I wanted to look. I hope that's okay."

I need to put her off a bit; if she leaves me alone, I'll be able to look around a little more closely and figure out how easy this place would be to break into.

I'm not sure if the fact that the owner is Eleanor's aunt is helpful or hurtful. Maybe I can glean information from Eleanor, but guilt stabs into me at the thought. I shove the feeling aside. Of course, the removal of the items will only be temporary, until I can get the items discovered. Preferably in the parents' possession.

"Of course, darling. Feel free to browse. I have some pieces to clean over here." She gestures to a corner station with cleaning supplies set up. "Just let me know if there's anything specific you want to look at, or if you have any questions."

"Thank you."

She turns her back to me and I take the opportunity to look around.

There's one camera in the corner, facing the front of the shop. The narrowness of the store works to their advantage, since the camera's angle should also capture a majority of the merchandise.

There's also a keypad next to the front door, indicating an alarm system, but I don't see any other evidence of security. I've seen similar setups before, though, and there's typically a keypad at every entrance or exit.

Since we're in a strip mall, I know there must be a rear entrance and parking in the back for employees. A doorway behind the counter probably leads there, but it's all shadowed and I can't tell if there's another keypad at the back door.

I drift closer to where Pearl is cleaning jewelry and clear my throat. "This time of week is always slow at my shop, too."

"Yes. Business should pick up over the weekend. More tourists up from Portland."

"True. My sister has to help with sales over the weekend." I chuckle. "Does Eleanor help you?"

"Me? No, no other employees. It's always been just me. Besides, Eleanor stays busy with her job at the library. Every now and then she helps me with my accounting, but that's about all she has time for. But I don't mind."

So it's not likely there will be any more cameras in the employee area. That might be the best way to come in, but I'll have to disable the alarm and then not get caught on camera. The keypad looks about a decade old and should be fairly simple to get by with nothing more than a magnet to deactivate the sensor at the door.

I gaze down into the case in front of me and realize it's full of diamond rings. The ones at the top are flashy, princess cut, at least three carats in platinum settings, and as my eyes roll down the case, the rings get increasingly modest.

More importantly, the case itself has a simple ratchet lock. It will be a snap to jimmy it open with only a few tools.

The bell over the door jangles and we both turn toward the sound.

"Buying me something nice?"

It's Jared.

Of course it is.

Because what guy wouldn't want to find his girlfriend of about one week standing in front of a bunch of engagement rings?

"I was just, uh, window-shopping."

"Window-shopping?" He stops next to me and glances down at the sparkly display case.

"Hello, Deputy, it's nice to see you again." Pearl dimples at Jared.

"Hey, Pearl. I see you've met my girlfriend, Ruby."

"Girlfriend?" Her eyes widen, swinging in my direction and shining with anticipation while her hands clasp together. "Is that why you're here, honey? Are you looking for rings?"

"What? No!" My face prickles with heat and I fan myself with one hand. "Is it hot in here?"

"I really like the emerald one, but I think the sapphire goes better with my eyes," Jared says.

There's a smile in his voice but I can't look at him. I'm too embarrassed.

"Thank you for letting me look around," I tell Pearl, simultaneously yanking Jared with me toward the exit.

"Are we going to check out cribs for our unborn children next?" Jared asks once we're outside on the sidewalk in the sunshine.

"I'm glad you find this so amusing." The words are muffled by my palms.

He tugs my hands away from my face with gentle fingers. "Hey, I'm just messing with you. You're allowed to look at jewelry without pledging your undying devotion to me for the rest of your days. Although I might not be completely against that either."

I laugh and shove him in the shoulder. "What are you doing here anyway?"

"I stopped at the post office on my way home." He gestures over his shoulder to the building. "I was just walking back to my car and happened to see you through the window. Don't think I didn't notice the subject change, by the way. Where's Paige?"

"She's at home. She's been pretty bored since Naomi left. We went to the movies today, and then I came out to just go for a walk. I invited her, but I don't think I'm cool enough to hang with all day."

Only partially true. I needed a chance to think about everything without Paige. I've involved her in enough, and even though she's a tough kid, the strain is wearing on her.

"Yeah, in the summer, most of the kids in town take off for Camp Umpqua up at the lake. There's not much to do here except go to the beach, and even that can get boring without friends."

I nod. "Have you had dinner?"

"Are you asking me on a date?" His brows lift.

"Only if you promise to put out afterward."

"I might be able to come up with something."

We smile, and for a second, everything is all right with the world.

"I'll pick something up and bring it over. Oh, that reminds me, I've got to run home first and grab my golf clubs. I promised your uncle I'd play with him tomorrow. We have an early tee time. I hope you don't mind if I wake you up early."

And then everything comes crashing back down to reality.

"Good. That's fine."

Except it's not good and it's not fine.

CHAPTER THIRTEEN

"How are things at work? Anything exciting happening lately?" I ask.

Two hours later, we're full of Chinese takeout, snuggling on the couch, watching *I Love Lucy* reruns, and chatting about random things. It's an odd ritual, having another adult around to just talk to about anything and everything.

Well, not everything.

We share funny stories about people we saw during the day, the show we're watching, and Paige. Plus the occasional theory about why Gravy still hisses at me at every turn.

"Nothing worth mentioning. Everything seems to be back to normal. The most excitement I've had this week was catching the Newsomes making out in the parking lot at the general store."

"You call that exciting?"

"Yeah, they must be off their game. They said they were," he grimaces, "*playing* in the park but someone was watching them. Mrs. Newsome thinks they're being trailed by a ninja." He laughs and shakes his head. "What about you? Any interesting readings? Anything involving a man in black?"

I cough a little to disguise my shock. Not only did the Newsomes see me, they *mentioned* seeing me. Hopefully they'll forget about it soon. "Not lately. Are you working tomorrow after golf with Uncle David?"

"Not until tomorrow night. After golf I'll probably run home and nap since I'm on call until at least two in the morning."

Good to know. I have plans the next night, and if Jared is on call, he won't be able to hang out. But I will have to keep an extra eye out for cruisers when I rob the jeweler's.

~*~

I spend the day working, playing cards with Paige, helping customers, balancing Ruby's accounts, and doing inventory.

For tonight, I won't need much, a small bag for my lock-picking tools, a magnet for the alarm, a can of black spray paint, and a flashlight.

The spray paint is a slight problem. I don't have any. If I purchase a can the same day of the robbery, it might lead back to me. So, I wait until Mr. Bingel and the boys have left for an errand to sneak into his garage and steal a can. Well, borrow. I plan on bringing it back tomorrow when I'm done with it.

I'm ready to go when I notice the shop phone has a message. The light is on. Weird, we don't get many calls outside business hours.

"Hey, Charlotte, it's Jackson Murphy."

Ruby's accountant.

"If you could call me back, I'd really appreciate it." He rattles off the number I already have on his business card and hangs up.

What does he need? The last thing *I* need is someone who knows I'm not Ruby showing up in town. Hopefully, he's just checking in.

I call him back, but it goes to voicemail. I leave a brief message, confirming I got his call and that I would be available for a couple hours.

Then I wait.

Waiting is the worst. I pace back and forth, dusting clean shelves and thinking too much. Gravy lies on the front counter, his crooked tail twitching back and forth while he watches me.

When it seems late enough that no one will be about—and too late to expect Jackson to call back—I grab my backpack full of tricks, lock the door behind me, and head out on foot.

Since I'm not tailing the parents again anytime soon, I brought Tabby her car back yesterday morning. Besides, it's not really necessary for the job tonight. Main Street is close enough for me to walk, staying in the shadows wherever possible. I'm wearing the same dark clothes I wore to tail the parents.

It's dark and quiet in Castle Cove at night. While everyone slumbers, I creep down to Main Street.

The back door to the jeweler's is almost too easy to sneak up on undetected, down a back alley flanked by the building itself on one side and tall leafy trees on the other.

I use the negative end of the magnet to locate the sensor in the door, sliding it in the crack of the frame until I feel the telltale tug. Then I flip it over and slip it into the crack, covering the sensor. After a final glance around, I click on the small flashlight and hold it in between my teeth, aiming it at the doorknob.

It only takes minutes to pick the lock. As soon as the tumblers fall, I swing open the door, my body tense in the darkness, and wait to make sure I haven't triggered the alarm.

After ten full seconds pass and everything remains silent, I slip inside.

The alarm isn't even set. It's not even a commercial model. It's a home model, outdated, and glowing a happy, unarmed green.

I let out a sigh and shake my head. What is wrong with these people and their trusting natures?

No time to relax. I dart to the adjoining door leading out to the shop and pause. I have to stay out of sight of the camera, but that won't be possible if I want to actually take anything of value.

Which means I need something to cover the lens.

This part might get tricky.

Keeping my back to the wall, I slide toward the camera, staying out of the range of the lens. When I'm directly underneath, I pull the spray can out of my bag and shake it, pushing the button once to test the nozzle.

Nothing happens.

I shake it and try again.

It's jammed.

Why didn't I check it before I left? That's like Robbery 101. I can hear Dad's uncompromising bellow in my head: *Check. Your. Damn. Gear.*

I need something else to cover the camera. I glance through the items in my bag. Nothing helpful there. Unless . . .

Slipping my black shirt over my head, I shake it out and then toss it underhand up and over the camera. It flutters against the lens and then slips to the floor.

Crap.

I reach out and snag my shirt, and then I try again.

And again.

And again.

I'm panting and sweating by the time the shirt hooks the top of the camera and covers the lens entirely.

I do a quiet victory dance in my bra before stalking over to the display case to get the goods.

Once again, I have to pick a lock. This one is smaller than the one on the door but less sophisticated. After a minute, it gives and I grab a dozen different items—tennis bracelets, rings, necklaces, and a few large diamond earrings—and shove them into my little black bag. For the coup de grâce, I pull out the mint toothpick from the parents' house and leave it on the ground next to the display case.

Then comes the hardest part. I have to get my shirt back down without getting in sight of the camera.

Using items at hand, I start throwing. A stapler swishes through the hanging fabric of my shirt and clatters to the ground. Then a small notebook.

I'm getting ready to throw my shoe when a light shines directly in the window, right at me.

CHAPTER FOURTEEN

Instantly, I plunge to the ground and huddle behind the counter, out of sight of the windows, praying to any and every deity in existence that I won't get caught here like this, in my bra, with a bag full of diamonds.

My heart is thumping so loudly in my ears I can't hear anything else.

The light is dancing on the wall behind me and then it suddenly veers off and disappears.

It was probably just someone driving by.

I'm an idiot.

Regardless, I stay in my hiding spot, waiting and listening, until the thumping of my heart subsides and everything remains dark and quiet.

Anxious to be done, I stand and move back out of sight of the camera before I continue throwing things to dislodge my shirt.

It takes longer than I want, but eventually it slips to the ground and I crawl over, out of sight of the lens, to retrieve it.

Once I have all my supplies in hand, I sneak back out the back door, making sure to retrieve the magnet as well. When I'm outside, I breathe a sigh of relief.

A cranky voice flies through the quiet night. "There's no one out here."

Stiffening, I press my back up against the wall, squeezing myself into the narrow shadow between the building and a Dumpster.

"I saw someone jumping around in there, I swear it."

Oh, no. I know that voice.

Mrs. Olsen. There's the squeaky sound of wheels against the pavement and then I see them.

They stop at the mouth to the alley underneath the illuminating cone of a streetlight. Mrs. Olsen is pushing Miss Viola in her completely unnecessary wheelchair. They're both in pajamas—button-up shirts and cotton pants, and they both have pink curlers in their hair.

What are they doing out this late?

"You're such a drama queen," Miss Viola says.

"I'm the drama queen? I'm not the one jumping off of cliffs in my unmentionables."

Miss Viola waves her hand. "That was forever ago."

"Two weeks is forever?"

"Would you quit your whining and get us back to the car?"

"You were the one who wanted to come outside at this godforsaken time of night." Mrs. Olsen lets go of the wheelchair to plant her hands on her hips.

"I can't help it, I needed fresh air. I've been having the hot flashes."

"Hot flashes? You went through menopause thirty years ago."

"It wasn't that long ago."

"Oh really, your dive into the ocean was forever ago, but menopause was just last week? You're deluded. It's not menopause, it's dementia."

"I'm not demented."

I cover my mouth with my hand to keep laughter from bursting out.

Mrs. Olsen jumps and lets out a startled shriek. "Did you see that? Something just moved."

"Nothing is there."

"I can see someone just standing there. Over by the garbage!" Mrs. Olsen flaps a hand, waving at her face. "I think I might pass out."

"You're fine. No one is there. It's your old eyes playing tricks. Why would anyone be skulking about the garbage in the middle of the night?"

"I don't know, maybe it's a robber."

"A robber of trash?"

"Maybe they're looking for something specific that people throw away, like underwear. I saw it on the news. There was a man in New York stealing people's used underwear."

"That didn't happen. And it's not stealing if it's in the garbage. Now let's go home and leave the panty thief to his own devices."

Mrs. Olsen grumbles, "So now you believe me about seeing someone stealing panties?" She starts walking again, so I don't hear Miss Viola's response. They head back down the street and I hold my breath until they're out of sight.

I wait a few extra minutes before leaving my hiding place.

I wish I could go home, but I'm not done yet.

It takes me about thirty minutes to walk to where the parents are staying. I ease a wedge into the top corner of the Mercedes's door to hold it open and then use a slender piece of crooked metal to click the release on the door lock without triggering the alarm. I've done this more than a few times and can break into a car faster than AAA. I click the trunk open and stash the little bag of jewels in the hidden compartment with the spare tire.

Slinking back home in the dark, I smile at my victory. Now it's just a matter of waiting for the robbery to be reported.

~*~

The next afternoon, I'm nearly dying of anticipation by the time Jared pops in with lunch.

And a surprise.

"What is that?"

"It's a bike for Paige." He rolls the bicycle into the shop. It's a nice, comfy-looking beach cruiser in pale blue with little skulls painted on it. "You were saying she's been bored since Naomi left so I thought this might cheer her up."

I can only shake my head at him. He's too much. "Where is she?"

"She went to the park with Mr. Bingel and the boys. They should be back soon."

He leans the bike against the wall and walks over to me. He leans across the register for a quick kiss. "I brought her a sandwich, too."

"I can put it in the fridge. She ate some cereal before she left for the park."

He pulls our lunch out of the plastic bag in his hand. "You know I really should teach you how to cook."

"I can cook."

"I mean something more than a bowl of cereal," he says, handing me my turkey sub.

"I'm an excellent mac 'n' cheese chef. And grilled cheese. And toast."

He rolls his eyes. "I stand corrected. When the zombie apocalypse hits, I'm immediately coming to your place."

"Because I'm awesome?"

"And because you have all the foods with the extra preservatives."

"Ha ha. I guess you can teach me some survival skills. I do like shocking Paige with handy new abilities." I unwrap my food and set it on the counter in front of me.

"What's her favorite food? One that doesn't come in a box," he clarifies.

I shrug. "Probably spaghetti."

"Good. That's easy enough. We'll start there."

We smile and give each other googly eyes, a move that would have made me sick a few months ago if I had witnessed it, but now it makes my stomach warm and fuzzy.

"How's your day going so far?" I ask, taking a bite of sandwich.

"Good. Same as always."

I try to school my features to remain neutral. But.

Same as always?

Really?

"Oh, there was one thing. I had an interesting call from Mrs. Olsen this morning."

"Oh?"

"Yeah. She and Miss Viola saw some guy in an alley spying on them. They seemed to think he was going to steal their unmentionables. And he was all in black, just like Mrs. Newsome's ninja at the park the other night."

"Strange. Do you think they really saw someone?"

He shrugs. "I don't know. It's weird two different people saw someone matching the same description creeping around. But Mrs. Olsen said the guy they saw was at least seven feet tall and looked like a pervert, even though they never saw his face. Also no crimes have been reported, so it might be nothing. What do you think? Do you know anything about this man in black? Have any gut feelings?"

My mouth opens, ready to give a negative reply, but then I pause. The robbery obviously hasn't been discovered yet; Jared would have said something if it had. I don't understand why, but I need to get it moving. The sooner the parents fall under some kind of suspicion, the better. Mother said she would buy me "a few more days," but that's vague, which means they could be showing up any day now.

"What is it?" he asks when I don't say anything right away.

"Where did Mrs. Olsen see this ninja guy?"

"Over behind the Main Street shops."

"Maybe you should check with the businesses over there. Maybe something is missing, but it hasn't been called in or noticed yet."

"You think so?"

I shut my eyes, making sure to furrow my brow with thought before I relax my face and then nod. "Yes."

It's weird that this time I'm the cause of the latest mystery in Castle Cove. One more thing to add to the guilt pile. Pretty soon, it's going to be big enough to crush me.

"Okay, I'll check it out."

We eat in companionable silence for a few minutes before Jared speaks again. "So Tabby and Troy's birthday party is Tuesday, did she tell you?"

"She did mention something about a bonfire on the beach."

"Yep. We've done the same thing every year since we were teens. There's music and drinks and lots of reminiscing about the good old days."

I wrinkle my nose. "The good old days? That makes you sound old."

He nudges me with a shoulder. "I am way older than you. And as your elder, I am demanding you come with me to the party. We'll bring tents and camp out on the beach afterward."

"Sounds fun. Can Paige come?"

"Of course. I have an extra one-person pop-up tent she can use."

"She'll love it. We've never been camping."

"Oh, and one more thing."

"You're really taking this bossy thing to a whole new level."

He rolls his eyes and keeps talking. "The gala for the library."

"Yeah, Eleanor mentioned it."

"You want to come with me? I'll wear a tux."

"When is the gala?"

"Next Friday night. It's fancy. I would buy you a dress for the event," he starts, holding up a hand when I open my mouth to protest. "But I knew you wouldn't like that, so I talked to Tabby and she said you could borrow one of hers. She's going, too, by the way, and she wants you to call her so you can get in on her evil plans. Her words, not mine."

"Okay." I smile.

"Okay," he repeats.

"Are you done planning the rest of our lives?" I roll my eyes and shake my head like I hate it, but inside I actually love it.

And then we do this really annoying lovebird thing where we sort of look at each other, smiling and happy, until he leans over and rubs the corner of my mouth with his thumb.

"You had some mustard." He puts his thumb in his mouth to suck it off and my body heats.

"Are you done eating?" I ask, a bit breathless.

"Yep." His eyes are intent and he pulls me toward him until we're pressed together. "You might be a little late reopening after lunch."

"A little late?" I feign disappointment.

"Maybe a lot late."

CHAPTER FIFTEEN

The next day, the robbery still hasn't been reported, despite someone seeing something fishy at the jewelry store, and despite the cops going to talk to Eleanor's aunt after I gave Jared my tip.

Why didn't she report anything missing?

I took quite a few items. Enough to notice, for sure.

Am I losing my mind? Was it all a dream? It couldn't have been. Mrs. Olsen and Miss Viola saw me, and that part was reported.

This is unacceptable. I've been lucky to buy a couple days from my parent's machinations, but they aren't going to wait much longer.

I don't want to go back to the scene of the crime, so instead I go to the library to dig for intel.

"Hey." I find Eleanor restacking books in the historical fiction section.

"Hey, you." She looks different, less buttoned-up perfection. Her hair isn't pulled back in her normal severe style. Instead, her blond waves are flowing over her shoulders, reaching nearly to the middle of her back. I didn't even realize her hair was so long. She's wearing her normal prim outfit but no pearls, and she's even got on lip gloss.

"You look nice."

She flushes a little. "Troy likes my hair down," she says, fingering a strand. "What brings you here?"

"Jared said we're all going to the gala and I wanted to ask you if you had to be there way early before the event? I thought maybe we could all go out to dinner together first somewhere nice since we'll all be dressed up."

"That would be awesome, but yeah, I have to be there about an hour before it starts to make sure all the vendors and everything check in on time, and I think we've hired Ben for the bar so he'll probably have to be there, too." She frowns.

"Well, that's okay, maybe some other time."

I totally knew it wouldn't happen, but I needed some kind of excuse to talk to Eleanor so I could casually bring up her aunt.

"Oh hey, I met your aunt the other day at the jewelry store."

It feels so scripted to me, but Eleanor doesn't seem to notice. "Aunt Pearl is the best. I've been helping her at the store when I can on the weekends, and sometimes after work."

"The store's been that busy?"

"Not really. But, you know, she's getting older and she keeps forgetting things." She shakes her head with a smile. "The other month she didn't pay the power bill and they almost shut it off. I found a whole stack of unpaid invoices in the desk drawer of her office." She sighs. "We're a little worried we're going to have to shut the place down soon if she gets worse. I had to redo her entire accounting . . ."

Eleanor keeps talking, but inside I'm dying. How am I supposed to pull off a robbery if the victim can't even recognize she's been robbed?

"Are you going to her store anytime soon?" I ask.

She grimaces. "I wish I could, but the preparations for the gala are taking up my whole life. Mrs. Smithson—the head librarian—should be helping me more, but she's having hip surgery in two weeks so everything has been falling to me. Although the Hamptons have been a huge help."

"I bet they have." I clench my jaw against a more sarcastic retort, inwardly screaming.

"The problem is they've been focused on obtaining the donors, not the back-end paperwork. Which just keeps growing."

Maybe that's why I haven't seen them since my little visit to their house the other morning. I mean, I've been avoiding them for sure, but they seem to be able to find me when they want anyway. They're probably preparing for a counterattack.

"I can help, too, if you need anything."

"Really?" Eleanor's face brightens. "That would be amazing. We'll definitely need help organizing the donations and keeping records of who is pledging what and all that. You would be a lifesaver, Ruby."

"It's no problem. I have to balance the books all the time at the shop, so I'm good at it. Let me know when you need me and I'll be here."

Plus it might give me access to some of my parents' information and this scam they're running. There has to be a way to get the money back to the people of Castle Cove once this is over.

But my current problem is more pressing than this farce of a charity ball. Someone needs to report the theft, and it can't be me.

~*~

I walk home, my thoughts buzzing. As I turn the corner by Mr. Bingel's house, I'm stopped in my tracks.

There's a sleek black sedan parked directly in front of Ruby's.

My heart stops for a long second before restarting in double time. Wait, it's not a Mercedes.

Is Ruby back? She's not due for nearly a month.

I duck behind a hedge and peer carefully through the leaves of the bush.

It's not Ruby. The owner of the sedan is standing on the porch, knocking at the door. The tall figure is dressed in a suit, his jaw angular and familiar.

It's Jackson Murphy, the accountant.

Crap. He never called me back after I returned his voicemail. I assumed it wasn't important. Except now he's here. *Why* is he here? What does he want? What could possibly be important enough to warrant a visit all the way to little Castle Cove?

I step out of my hiding place to find out, but I'm too late. Before I've made it more than a couple steps, he jogs back to the car, slides in, and pulls away.

"Were you playing hide-and-go-seek?" a little voice asks.

I jump a foot in the air. "Gary. You scared the crap out of me." I press a hand to my chest.

His mouth drops open. "You said crap," he whispers.

"I know. I'm sorry."

He shrugs. "That's all right. Sometimes, when we're driving with Mr. Bingel, he calls people jack rabbits."

I nod. "It's easy to get angry while you're driving."

"Do you want to play hide-and-seek with me?" His eyes are wide and innocent and I can't possibly say no.

Thirty minutes later, I jog up the front steps to find a note taped to the front door.

Charlotte, it reads. *I have business nearby, but I'll be back in town next Saturday. Hopefully we can chat then.*

It's signed with his initials.

Saturday.

The day after the gala.

I rub my head with one hand and crumple the note with the other. I don't have time for this. That's less than a week away.

CHAPTER SIXTEEN

"You were right again. There was a theft at one of the shops on Main Street. Right by where Miss Viola and Mrs. Olsen saw their ninja."

Finally.

We're at Ruby's and Jared is showing me how to make spaghetti.

"What happened?" I keep my eyes on the sauce I'm stirring on the stove.

"Someone stole a whole ream of jewels from Pearl, Eleanor's aunt." He rustles around in the fridge behind me.

"Oh, no."

The fridge shuts. "I went and talked to everyone on Main Street after you mentioned it might be helpful, but she didn't tell me anything was missing. Then Eleanor went over there today and . . . Apparently Pearl's been having some cognitive difficulties. They don't even know how long it's been gone, if it's actually been stolen or just misplaced." He sighs and bends over to pull out some pots from one of the cabinets.

"That's horrible. Poor Pearl."

"It gets worse. One of the pieces taken was a family heirloom. Pearl must have accidently put it in the display. Eleanor is panicked. It's supposed to be her wedding ring. It belonged to her great-great-great-grandmother or something."

Oh, shit.

I have to get those items back to her.

I *will* get them back to her, and take the parents down at the same time. Win win.

"Did they find anything else? Any clues about who might have done it?" I ask, still stirring but my body half turned in his direction so I can enjoy the view.

He fills a pot with water and sets it on the stove. "Nope. Anything that might give an indication of who it was, prints, all that has been wiped away by now."

And probably the toothpick has been moved or thrown away, too.

Dammit.

I'll have to come up with another way to implicate them.

"Do they have an alarm or surveillance? You'd think a jewelry store with that kind of inventory . . ."

"They do, but it's outdated. The alarm would be easy to bypass anyway, but Eleanor said Pearl hasn't been setting it because she keeps forgetting her code. And the video recycles every twenty-four hours. We went through everything available and there's nothing."

"What are you going to do?"

"I'll have to work tonight. The chief wants to increase patrolling in the area, just in case. Keeping an eye out for this ninja person." He rolls his eyes. "How does the sauce look?"

"Saucy."

He sidles up next to me and takes the spoon from my hands, stirring once before getting a small taste in the cup of the spoon. "The most important part of cooking is sampling the goods. To make sure it's not poisonous." He holds up the spoon, blowing on it gently before turning the sauce in my direction.

I close my lips around it and watch his neck pulse when he swallows in time with me.

"Mmmm."

His eyes are fixed on my mouth. "Is it good?"

"Very good," I say. "I'm never going to be able to cook as well as you can."

"Then it's a good thing I'm not planning on going anywhere."

My heart sinks a little. He might be here to stay, but I am not. Something must flicker in my expression, though, because he puts the spoon down and envelops me in his arms. He tugs me against his chest.

We stand there for a second, his chin on my head and my head against his chest, listening to his heartbeat.

"You know you can trust me, right?"

He's said these exact words before. A few times. More than a few times.

The boiling water bubbles over, making the stove hiss, and I jump in his arms.

He chuckles and then releases me, turning to the stove to turn down the heat. After he opens the package of fresh noodles and drops them into the water, he turns back and grabs my waist, pulling me against him. "Are you going to miss me while I'm working all night?"

"Maybe." I pretend indifference.

He thwaps my butt and then turns back to the stove. "The noodles will be ready quick. Will you get the strainer?"

"Sure." I open the cupboard and reach up for the colander, then frown as I pull it down. It feels heavy, like there's something in it.

I set it on the counter in front of me. There's a black velvet bag inside of the strainer.

My heart nearly stops.

My velvet bag.

The one I used to store the jewelry that I stole and planted on the parents. It's here.

This is no coincidence.

My heart sets up a dull thud in my chest. Thankfully, Jared is still stirring the sauce, his back to me.

I can't just grab the bag and shove it down my pants. The jangling would be too loud, and the bag would be too obvious.

Panicked, I scan the cupboard for something to mask the noise. There are a few nesting bowls on the middle shelf, fairly thick and heavy. It will have to do.

I reach up and brace myself. With one hand, I cover the jewelry bag. With the other hand, I tip the bowls back toward me. Simultaneously, I grab the jewels, shoving them into my pants while letting the bowls fall, crashing noisily onto the counter. They don't break, but the resulting bang is enough to cover the sound of the jangling in my shorts.

"Are you okay?" Jared's next to me almost immediately, righting the bowls now spread all over the counter.

"Yep," I squeak and then clear my throat.

This is so not going to work.

"That scared me. I'm so clumsy today." I laugh.

We put the bowls back up in the cupboard and I hand him the colander.

"Um, I'll be right back. Bathroom break." Careful not to jostle the jewels hiding in my underwear, I leave the kitchen.

When I'm out of hearing range, I run up the stairs. The only place I can think to put them is under the loose board in the floor of Ruby's room. I check the bag first. Everything I took is still in there.

The parents somehow put the loot back on me. And they timed it with precision.

Now what am I going to do with them? I don't have time to put them back in the parents' possession. I can't keep them here. They're probably trying to find a way to frame me, like I tried to do to them. I have to get them back to Pearl and Eleanor.

But I can't sneak back to the store either. Jared just told me they'll be running extra patrols at night looking for the ninja. A.k.a. me.

I've got to take them somewhere else. Anywhere else that can't be traced back to me. And I've got to do it as soon as possible, before they find a way to pin it on me.

CHAPTER SEVENTEEN

One thing is certain: someone other than me has to find the jewels. And it has to be soon.

The perfect opportunity presents itself the very next night—Troy and Tabby's birthday party.

Thank god for parties on Tuesdays.

Since it's going to be on the beach, it should be a snap to lead someone to the jewels. The hard part is going to be hiding them to begin with, somewhere they won't be found until I want them to be.

The party will be held near the pier, in a secluded spot that also has some picnic tables and barbeques.

When Jared calls me the afternoon of the party, I immediately volunteer to help set up chairs and hike the food and drinks down to the beach.

And Paige will be there to help me run a distraction.

I close up the shop at four, and Jared meets us at Ruby's, his Jeep already packed with tents, sleeping bags, coolers and lanterns.

Paige is ecstatic. We've never camped anywhere before, let alone on the beach.

"This is going to be awesome," she says as we're stuffing our small bags and towels in the back of Jared's Jeep. "Will you show me how to light a fire, like the real way without matches and stuff?"

"Sure," Jared replies.

She continues to pepper him with questions while we get into the car and drive down to the beach.

I have the bag of jewels tightly wrapped to avoid jangling and shoved into the deep pocket of the cargo shorts I picked out this morning.

I'll have to plant them quickly, as soon as we get there, to avoid detection. The second Jared gets too close, he's going to feel the lump.

He parks in a small lot next to the pier and we carry items down to the beach. Jared and I take the larger items, and we have Paige carry the presents. We got funny T-shirts made for them. Troy's says *World's Okayest Police Officer* and the one for Tabby reads *This is What Winners Look Like*.

We set everything up in a small area with picnic tables and grass and barbeques next to a large expanse of sand leading down to the beach.

There aren't many people around, probably because it's a Tuesday. Just a few stragglers who are packing up for the day. Eleanor will be showing up in about an hour, after her shift at the library ends, and Ben should be here any minute to help finish getting everything ready before the birthday twins arrive.

We leave the coolers by one of the picnic tables in the shade and Jared cleans off the barbeque while he has Paige find the best, flattest spot for the tents.

I wait until he's busy showing her how to set the tent up. "I'm going to find the bathroom," I call out. There were a few Sani-Huts up at the parking lot, so once Jared waves to acknowledge he heard me, I head out in that direction. Once I'm out of sight, I veer toward the pier.

It should be pretty easy to lure Jared away from the party later with the excuse of making out under the stars. I need to find a spot I can easily locate later, but where no one else will find the jewels before we get there.

It's quiet and dark under the pier. The only sound is the splash of the waves against the wooden beams and the faraway squawk of seagulls.

I scan the area, looking for a good place to lure Jared. It can't be too damp, and it should be close, somewhere it will be natural to make out.

I pick the closest beam and pull the bag out, unwrapping it to make it as big and jangly as possible. Then I put the jewels down in the sand, right up against the wood, and cover the bag with a thin layer of sand.

That will have to do.

~*~

A few hours later, the sun is setting while the guys try to show Paige how to light a fire without matches and lighter fluid.

Key word being "try."

Since Tabby insists no one over fifty is allowed, the party consists of Paige, Jared, Ben, Tabby, Troy, Eleanor . . . and me. And that's it.

"There's really no one else under fifty in town?" I ask Tabby.

"It doesn't matter, Mrs. Olsen always crashes anyway."

Eleanor and I laugh.

Eventually, the fire gets started with matches instead of the manly skills that weren't working, and Tabby brings out an old boom box. Some kind of old-school disco music fills the space around the fire, along with some impromptu dancing and laughing. Ben teaches Paige how to do the hustle while Jared and Troy argue over who's the best Boy Scout and Tabby and Eleanor make drinks.

Once darkness falls, voices approach.

"Oh, what's going on here?" The voice is full of calculated surprise.

"Mrs. Olsen," Tabby groans. "I told you, this is a kids-only party."

"You are hardly a child."

"I'm more of a child than you are."

"Well, that's certainly true. I just happened to be in the area."

"Of course," Tabby mutters.

"Why, Mrs. Olsen, fancy running into you here." It's Mr. Godfrey. "I was just taking a moonlit walk on the beach," he booms.

He's not alone.

Apparently, everyone in Castle Cove just happened to be walking out on the beach tonight, because within minutes, our little party has turned into a much bigger affair.

Tabby groans and protests and pretends to be put out, but secretly I think she loves the tradition.

It works to my advantage as well because as soon as everyone is distracted, I make it over to Jared's side and whisper in his ear.

"I've always wanted to have sex on the beach."

He goes completely still, and then his hand grips mine and we're dashing away from the fire.

"This way," I tug him toward the pier.

This could be so romantic. I would be more turned on if the whole thing weren't a deception.

Giggling to mask my anxiety and guilt, I lead him over to the pier, near the beam where I hid the jewels.

Except the tide is rising.

The waves haven't covered the spot with the jewels yet, but they're getting close. Too close. Too close for me to use the spot as a place to get frisky. I have to think of another way.

And fast, because if I wait too much longer, they'll be washed out to sea.

I can't let that happen to Pearl.

And then Jared's mouth covers mine in the darkness, his warm hands framing my face, and for a minute the jewels and everything else completely disappear.

We sink into the cool sand together, and I try to gather my wits about me, but Jared's hands are strong and familiar. His scent envelops my senses, making the world feel suddenly like home and comfort.

He pulls back for a second, his eyes trying to see me in the darkness under the pier, where even the moon barely shines through the slats.

"I love you." He breathes the words into me, and before I can respond, his mouth covers mine and I completely forget about the jewels and where we are and the sand getting into my clothes and everything else.

It's not until the surge has ended and we're both getting dressed that I have time to think about what he said. He loves me? The real me, or the fake me? Do I even know the real me? He didn't give me a chance to say the words back. Would I have? Should I have? Is it wrong to say it, even if it's true, if it's said in a moment of deception? They're all moments of deception.

Dammit, the jewels!

I walk over to the wooden post where I know the jewels are. The waves are touching the tip of the bag. I can barely make out the inky black material against the lighter-colored wet sand.

So close.

I bend over and pretend to use the water to rinse off my hands and wait. Hoping. Knowing as I know my own heartbeat that Jared will follow me here, hating myself for using him, hating that he used this moment to whisper words I've never heard from any man in my life.

His footsteps ruffle the sand behind me.

I turn and lean into him, kissing him while pressing him back in the direction I need him to go.

He steps back and then falters.

Gotcha.

"What . . ." He leans down and picks up the bag.

"What is that?" I ask, pulling back from him.

"I'm not sure." He shakes it and brushes it with his hands to get the dirt off and then opens it, feeling inside. "It feels like jewelry." His voice is bewildered.

"Jewelry? I wonder how it got out here." I flavor my voice with astonishment.

"It's . . . really very strange. Come on." His voice suddenly brisk, he takes my hand and we leave the haven of the dark pier for the circle of light around the bonfire, where the party has doubled in size since we left.

Jared takes me over to one of the picnic tables, where Tabby and Eleanor are arm wrestling. He drops a quick kiss on my lips before leaving in search of Troy, presumably, the jewel bag still clasped in his hand.

A few minutes later, they're both heading away from the beach, toward Jared's Jeep. He'll probably have to call it in to Anderson, who's on duty tonight.

I try to focus at least part of my attention on Tabby and Eleanor, who are now thumb wrestling for some reason, but I can't help but feel guilty and also a bit paranoid.

Is it all too obvious? Does Jared know, or suspect, the truth? Or some version of it?

CHAPTER EIGHTEEN

The first rule of running a con is simple: don't get too close.

I've already broken that rule many times over.

The second rule is always be prepared. There, I have some success.

"Ruby." Eleanor calls the shop the day after I've realized I'm the worst human being on the planet. Possibly the galaxy.

"Hey, Eleanor."

"You know how you said you could help with some of the charity gala stuff? Do you think you could come by this afternoon? We have so many people promising donations that the paperwork is getting completely out of hand."

"Of course. I can be there around three, if that's okay."

The bell over the shop door jangles and I glance up from the counter.

It's a thirty-something couple I don't recognize. Must be tourists. I smile and wave at them before getting back to my conversation.

"That would be perfect," Eleanor says. "I need help going through the paperwork and organizing the volunteer duties for the night of the event. Tabby said she would help, too."

"Awesome."

We chat a little longer before I make my excuses, since there are customers in the store.

"Is there anything I can help you with?" I ask.

The couple looks over from the bookcase full of information on everything from healing herbs and crystals to interpreting auras.

"You've got an interesting store here," the man says.

He's on the short side, just a few inches taller than his wife. But he's stocky, like he works out a lot. In fact, her arms look fairly toned, too. Maybe they're health-nut types. And I'm assuming she's his wife because they're both wearing rings. They're also wearing Castle Cove T-shirts I recognize from one of the stores on the boardwalk.

"Thank you. Is there anything I can help you find?" I repeat my earlier question.

"No. We're just looking around." He glances around at the words.

The conversation and the couple are innocuous enough, but it's an act. And not a very good one.

"Okay. I'll be up at the counter. Just let me know if you have questions."

I smile and walk back to the register, pretending to balance the books, but really I'm watching the customers.

They're too quiet. They don't act like a married couple; there's no shared glances or laughs or touches . . . although, who knows, maybe they hate each other. I don't have time to dwell on them though because the bell over the door rings, and the parents walk in hand in hand, smiling and laughing with each other. Further proof it's impossible to tell what people are like, what a relationship is like when you're looking from the outside.

"Hello, darling," Mother says, her voice happy, her face smiling for our audience.

"Hello," I say brightly.

Without breaking eye contact, I move my hand under the counter, trailing my fingers until they reach the recorder's on switch. The movement is familiar and instinctive by now.

The tourist woman stops before making her exit, her eyes flicking over the parents before she follows her husband out the door.

Once the door shuts behind them, Mother drops the act, her mouth flattening.

I expect them to rail at me for the whole trying-to-frame-them-with-stolen-jewelry thing, but they don't.

"I suppose it would be too much to ask that you've gotten better information from your little boyfriend," Father says.

"So we won't ask." Mother hands me a folder.

I'm almost scared to open it.

But I can't avoid it.

The first item is a categorized list, things I've done mixed with things they've done on my behalf, all typed and bullet-pointed for ease of reading.

Underneath, they've listed more info to back up the list. Articles about the real Ruby and her very much living family, a glossy print of me planting the bag of jewels under the pier in broad daylight, and a document linking Jared's account to an account in my name. Not Ruby Simpson, but "Charlotte Hampton." They even gave me their current last name.

This is not good.

The folder is snapped out of my hands.

Father is smiling, the expression smug.

Mother is severe, her lips in a straight line. "The gala is our last night here. There will be a lot of donations made during the auction. You have until nine o'clock on Friday night. If you don't—"

Father puts a hand on her shoulder.

She smiles at him, though the meek expression never reaches her eyes, before turning back to face me. "You know what to do."

With one last parting look, they leave.

I'm thankful the shop is empty for the moment. I shut off the recorder and then close my eyes to think.

Well. At least that's one more thing I can use to show who they really are. Too bad it implicates me as well if the cops ever get ahold of it.

It might be enough to prevent them from double-crossing me and Paige, but it's not enough to stop the scheme they have rolling now.

There's only one real option left.

It's the only way to keep Paige—and Castle Cove's coffers—safe from them.

I have to turn them in, which means I have to turn myself in, too.

But first, I have one last angle to work. Maybe there's something in their secret safe, something even slightly incriminating that I can use against them. I have to try.

Either way, this is going to be the end for me.

I have to look Jared in the eye and tell him the truth, about every deception, every lie, every betrayal. I'm going to jail. But I don't matter anymore.

The only thing that's ever mattered is Paige.

~*~

I make it to the library just after three. A teenager running the front desk directs me to a room in the back.

I have to go through a door marked *Employees Only* and then down a darkened hallway, following the light coming out of an open doorway.

"Oh good, you're finally here," Tabby says. The room isn't necessarily small, maybe the size of Ruby's shop, but floor-to-ceiling bookshelves stacked with books line the walls. Reams of paper and office supplies litter the floor. Most of the center of the room is taken up by a massive table surrounded by decrepit plastic chairs with metal legs, the same kind I had to sit in during Paige's parent-teacher conference. Something I won't be doing ever again, if all goes to plan. But Paige will still be sitting in these damn uncomfortable chairs for a while yet. I'm going to make sure of it.

"This place is like a prison." Tabby pushes a stack of papers in my direction. "You get to do the heavy lifting. I'm going to work on the donation list."

"Where's Eleanor?" I glance down at the papers she's heaved at me. They look like bank statements.

"She had to help a customer or something." Tabby dismisses the question with a wave.

I sit down across from Tabby and glance over the statements, shuffling through some of the papers. "What are these?"

"They're proof of deposits from the Hamptons, and receipts for donations. We're just copying the information onto a ledger to make sure the final balance matches what we're sending to each charity. The receipts have the names of the charities. Then there's a list of people who signed up for the dinner, fifty bucks per plate. So those deposits go on the other list so we can make the place cards for the dinner. I think we've got over two hundred people attending. They wanted us to do the accounting for a sort of checks and balances, to make sure nothing gets missed. Isn't that awesome?"

"So very awesome." And clever.

By involving the donating citizens in this way, the parents have pretty much assured no questions will be asked. And no one will ever know if the charities actually get the money or not. No one would have cause to be suspicious. After all, Tabby and Eleanor are going through the books at the Hamptons' behest.

I have to unclench my teeth and focus on the positive. The bank account is in both of their names. They're using a New York address, one I recognize as a fake. The important part is in the top right: the account number. I'm sure it's a front.

As I copy numbers and receipts over into the ledger—what a waste of time—I think about ways to get the parents out of the house so I have enough time to break into their safe. What if I arrange some kind of get-together for the charity, but then I can't make it? A dinner or something to keep them tied up for a couple of hours so I know they won't be home. I can act like I'm going and flake out at the last minute. It would help if I could get it set up somewhere far enough away to give me extra time if I need it.

A swishing sound makes me look up. Tabby's feet are up on the table and she's filing her nails.

The picture makes me smile. I hate to use her like this, but it's not like I have much of a choice. "I thought you were going to work on the donations?"

"I am. I'm thinking. We already have some, but I really think we need more. Hey, you wanna donate a free reading or something?"

"Sure."

"Sweet. Do you think you could get Jared to donate something, too?"

"What would he donate?"

She shrugs and sets the nail file on the table. "I don't know." She stews for a few seconds and then her face brightens. "Oh, maybe a lap dance."

I tilt my head at her. "Really?"

"You know how they have those strippers who dress up like cops and then pretend to arrest someone, and they're like," she deepens her voice, " 'You are under arrest . . . for being so hot' and then they strip off their clothes and get all crazy?" She nods. "He could totally do that."

"What about Troy? He could strip, too."

"What? Gross. No one wants a strip tease from that lug of meat."

"Sure they do, everyone but you."

She winces. "Don't tell me you would want one from him."

"Nah, I already have my own lug of meat. What about you? You could donate something."

She purses her lips. "I would totally offer a lap dance but so many people would bid it might cause a riot."

I laugh. "Not a lap dance, but you could offer some handyman-type skills. Handy*woman*-type skills."

"True." She picks up her emery board again, peering at her nails. "Ben's already doing an open bar at the gala, but I could probably get him to donate something, too. My list isn't long enough. We need more people involved."

My ears prick up. Here's my chance. "You could go around to the local business and ask for donations."

Her nose wrinkles. "That sounds terrible and it would take forever. You know how the people in this town like to chat. It would take me a week just to get through the shops on one side of the boardwalk. We don't have the time. We only have two more days."

"You could just send a letter or call."

"Too informal. People here are weird about that. If you're asking them for money, you should have the manners to do so while looking them in the eye."

"Maybe the Hamptons will have an idea," I say. "They've done this kind of thing before."

"True. I've been meaning to bring them a casserole or something, to welcome them to town, but I'm not sure if they like that kind of thing."

"They seem too fancy for casseroles." The bait is loaded into the trap.

"You're right. Hey," she snaps her fingers, "maybe I can invite them over for dinner."

And it's taken.

"That's a great idea," I say, injecting enthusiasm into my voice. "And maybe some of the other local business owners, too. Get them all in one spot at a set date and time for a scheduled event so you don't have to track them down and get stuck in conversation all day, but you can still look them in the eye while you have your hand out."

She's nodding slowly.

"I'll help you clean and prepare your house. We might have to move some furniture around . . ."

"Ugh. My house is way too small for something like that."

"Yeah, mine, too. Maybe Troy's?" I suggest.

"No way. He's the worst host ever. We'd all be using paper plates and plastic sporks from the general store deli."

I nod and glance down at the statements in front of me, shuffling through them and writing down some more numbers while she's thinking.

Finally, it hits her. "You should totally convince Jared to have it at his place. It's super nice and big enough for everyone. Tell him we'll cook."

I laugh. "He'll never let us cook. He'd worry we'd burn the place down or serve peanut butter and jelly sandwiches."

"He would be correct to worry. Which is why it's the perfect solution. He'll do everything for us."

"Probably. That would make me feel bad, though. I don't want to take advantage of our relationship." Even though that's exactly what I'm doing.

"Well, I have no problems using Jared for personal gain. I'll ask him first. If he says no you can butter him up and convince him. And by butter him up, I mean sex. Make him happy and thinking with the small head so the big head has no chance of refusing." She nods sagely.

"Got it."

CHAPTER NINETEEN

It's easier than I thought to get Jared to agree to do the dinner at his place. The same day we discuss it, Tabby calls him to ask if we can use his house and he immediately agrees.

It's almost too easy. I don't have to butter him up at all.

And we don't even have to cook because the Hamptons graciously agree to have the dinner catered.

How generous.

Although I have to admit, it is helpful in getting the dinner party organized quickly, since time is of the essence. There are only two more days until the gala, and the donors for the silent auction are one of the most important parts of the night. It's the last thing to be sorted out and poor Eleanor is beside herself with anxiety over the whole thing. I'm suffering from the same affliction. This is my one opportunity to get something to use against the parents.

I hate the thought of leaving the parents to their own devices with Jared, but what else can I do? I watch them drive to Jared's on the tracking device, and I wait until I know they're there before I call him.

"Hey, I'm going to miss dinner tonight."

"What's going on?"

"Paige is sick." I already told her to stay home and out of sight for a day or two.

"Do you need me to bring you anything?"

"No, she's just got a cold. Fever. You know, kids are resilient. She'll probably be better by tomorrow but I don't want to leave her. Tell Tabby and Eleanor I'm really sorry. I know you guys will be able to handle it without me, though."

"It will be hard but I guess we'll survive."

"Call me when everyone leaves?"

"Of course."

We hang up.

I pack a small bag of essentials, then ride Paige's new bike to where the parents are staying.

Instead of being sneaky and dressed in black, I park right on the side of the driveway and walk up like I belong here.

I know this town. Neighbors in these kinds of residential areas are nosy and suspicious. If I act like I'm supposed to be here, they'll think it's true. Plus everyone already thinks I'm their niece. If I go slinking around and someone spots me, no doubt there will be yet another ninja story. I can't afford to attract any more suspicion.

It doesn't take long to jimmy the lock with my kit and then I'm in. I head upstairs to the office, to where I saw the safe the last time I was here.

Even without clicking on the lights, I can tell it's not here. I check under the desk, in the small closet that's also in the office, and nothing.

Then I double-check all the rooms upstairs, looking under the beds in each one. Nothing. The safe is small, but not small enough to hide in a drawer or something. I check out the downstairs, every closet I can find, the garage, anywhere else I can think of.

It's not here.

There's only one other possible place they could be keeping it.

In their car.

Which is at Jared's, where I just called and made excuses *not* to be.

Dammit.

After making sure I've left everything as it was, I leave the house and lock the front door on my way out.

It takes forty-five minutes to bike to Jared's. My legs are burning by the time I get there. I park on the main road and head in, walking near his driveway but in the woods, somewhat sheltered from view by the trees and bushes.

By the time I reach Jared's driveway, it's full dark. The lights are on in his house, and voices spills out from the backyard.

The parents' car is near the front, close to the house.

I peer inside the window. It's unlocked.

How could they be so careless? They have been acting more and more out of character. Sloppy, even.

Letting out a breath, I peer into the back seat—it's not there. I open the driver-side door and pop the trunk.

Got it.

It's heavy, but I manage to pull it out and put it on the ground before gently shutting the trunk. Then I carry it into the nearest part of the woods, walking far enough away that the glow from the flashlight will be somewhat shielded from the house. I put the safe down and drop to a comfortable seat in front of it.

I put the flashlight on the ground, aimed at the safe, and then pull out the rare-earth magnet, which I have wrapped in a sock.

I place the magnet to the left and just above the keypad lock and jerk on the handle of the safe. It takes less than five seconds.

The lock pops open with a satisfying click and I slowly pull the lid open.

There's a bound stack of bills and a few jewelry cases. Underneath, two manila envelopes, one thicker than the next. I was sort of expecting something like Blackbeard's treasure or maybe human skulls. I don't know, something more nefarious.

Heart thumping, I pick up the flashlight in one hand and one of the envelopes in the other.

In the first envelope, the thinner of the two, there's a birth certificate for an Andrea Winchester.

The parents are listed as Mary and John Winchester. The birthdate is January fifth, thirteen years ago.

I put it to the side and open up the second, thicker envelope. Court documents. Some kind of trust. I scan the pages of legal jargon until I reach the name of the beneficiary. Andrea Winchester. I flip to the back of the documents, searching for a list of items held in trust. It's pages and pages of bank accounts, properties, vehicles . . . Skimming back through the document, I find a section stating that the money and items listed will become available to Andrea Winchester when she reaches her majority, age eighteen.

As the voices and laughter at Jared's filter through the forest, my heart beats a fast tattoo in my chest. I can't push for more time. What I've found is enough for now. It has to be. Hurriedly, I stuff the items back in the safe and then carry it back to their car. I place it back in the exact spot I found it and then shut the trunk.

Racing back to the bike, only one thought thumps through my mind.

Paige isn't my sister.

CHAPTER TWENTY

When I get home, Paige is in the living room, curled up on the couch. The TV is on but the volume is low. I immediately want to go to her, but I have to check out something first.

I call out a greeting to let her know I'm back, and then I jog upstairs to the office.

There's some important research to be done.

Thirty minutes later, I sit back in the chair. I have what I need. It was easy to find. John Winchester was part of a very large, very wealthy family. He married Mary Turner and they had a daughter, Andrea. They left Andrea at home for the first time with a babysitter to fly to New York City for a dinner and a show, their first date since the baby was born, the article states. They never returned home—they both died in a plane crash on the way back. It was a small private plane. Andrea was only a few months old. By all accounts, they were a loving couple and their death a tragic accident.

There's a black-and-white picture of an attractive and well-dressed couple. Very old money, given the clothes and jewels.

It was all over the news after they died, coming from such a prominent family. Also briefly mentioned was how all of their assets were tied up in trust for their infant daughter.

There were other articles, more numerous than the ones about John and Mary's death. Only a couple weeks after they died, someone kidnapped Andrea Winchester. The family mounted an extensive search, but she was never found.

Updates come in a few a year, articles from local papers with pictures of what Andrea might look like today.

She looks like Paige.

I dig up more information on the rest of the Winchester family. John and Mary had a few siblings, some with kids of their own. The pictures I find online are of happy, smiling families. There are articles about charity work as well as their continued search for Andrea. Not much else, but it's enough.

Paige has a family. A real family. One that doesn't lie, cheat, or steal for a living. A family that could take care of her better than I have.

A little voice in my head quakes at the thought. *But they don't know her. Not like I do.*

My eyes water and I shut them against the implications of everything I know and everything I have to do.

Keep Paige safe.

I trudge back down the stairs. What does the future hold? Do I really have any control over any of it?

"Hey." I sit on the couch next to her. "What are you doing?"

"Just hanging out." She's in her pajamas, some new ones covered in a rainbow zebra print. I bought them a few weeks ago, when Tabby and I were in Roseburg. When I saw them, I had to get them, despite our lack of funds. It was worth a few extra readings past closing for the next week to pay for them. She's always had a weakness for zebra anything, and she squealed at the soft, luxurious feel of the fabric.

Her hair is braided back from her face and she looks so incredibly young. Too young. I can't tell her about everything I've found. I don't even know where to start. I've barely been able to process the information myself. I will tell her, but not yet.

With everything that's been going on, I've barely seen her. I've been so focused on protecting her and taking down the parents that I haven't been able to spend time just talking with her.

"Are you okay?"

She shrugs.

"It's going to be all right, Paige. I promise."

"You can't know that."

But with this new information, I finally have a glimmer of hope. Maybe it will be all right. For Paige. She isn't their daughter. Which means they don't have a legal right to her, and maybe I can protect her. I don't quite know how they did it. How did they find her? How did they take her? I could swear Mother had a pregnant belly before Paige was born. I was only seven or eight, but I remember her being pregnant. Did they fake the whole thing to steal this orphan with a trust fund? And now they need her to cash out when she turns eighteen? Is that why they're protective of her and trying to use me to pay off whoever is after them? So they can get access to her trust fund in five years? Talk about a long con.

Although it's not like it's been hard for them to raise another child. They had me as a babysitter, after all.

I watch her while she watches TV. Her dark hair is like mine, except hers is darker. I always thought we had matching noses, but now that I'm really looking, hers ticks up slightly at the end. We both have full mouths, but my bottom lip is slightly smaller than the top, whereas hers are both wide and full.

Did I always just see what I wanted to see?

"Do you remember the time I took you to the mall when we were living in Illinois?"

It was one of the smallest towns we lived in. It was the one place where we could walk to the shopping center when our parents weren't around to stop us.

One corner of her mouth ticks up. I've told her this story before.

"We were walking along, and I stepped on a fruit loop someone had dropped on the ground. You looked over at me and whispered, 'You're a cereal killer.'"

We laugh.

"You were so clever. Even at five."

"You were practically my age." She smiles. "But I kept calling you Mom."

I chuckle at that. "I got some weird looks from people that day."

"You *were* basically my mom." Paige shrugs. "You still are."

"I know," I say softly.

It doesn't matter to me if Paige isn't my real sister. She's mine in every other way.

We sit there and watch TV together in silence, except I'm not watching whatever's happening on the screen. I'm thinking.

I've already decided how to save her. And the town. But it means giving up everything. And in order to pull it off, I have to make sure Paige is safe until everything can be brought to light, which means she has to be away from here. If my suspicions are correct and the parents are conning me so they can keep Paige and her trust fund while trying to pay off their big-shot attorney buddy who also sells people on the side, she's not safe here.

I turn to face her.

Making a deal with a teenage girl is like swimming with sharks. Minus the cage.

"You're not going to like this, but I need to hide you somewhere safe."

~*~

The day of the gala is bright and sunny. Thunderbolts and storm clouds would be more appropriate, though, something to match the anxiety building in my stomach. After the gala, I'm staying the night with Jared and that's when everything is going to change.

I'm going to tell him the truth.

It's not going to be easy. As a matter of fact, it's going to suck. He's probably going to have to arrest me, and I'm going to let him. He's already promised me once that he'll take care of Paige, and if I give him the information about who Paige really is, he's going to make sure the parents can't take her.

At least, that's my hope.

But I've got to get through the day and the gala first. I have to give my parents what they want in order to placate them, then drop the bomb on Jared before they can get away.

The morning goes by quickly, mostly because I spend it driving. I borrow Mr. Bingel's 1979 Buick. I take Paige to the only place I can think of where she'll be safe and looked after and no one will find her until I tell them where she is. More hopes.

We leave early and I don't get back into town until the afternoon.

When I pull the car into Mr. Bingel's driveway, Tabby is waiting for me.

"Where have you been? We've got plans, sister!"

I dodge her question by asking her about dinner the night before and pray she's too distracted to ask about Paige, but if she does, I'll just keep up with the sickness excuse.

We head to Eleanor's house to get ready.

On the way there, Tabby relays what happened at Jared's during dinner the night before, all the finalized plans for the gala and how they've gotten a bunch more people to donate their time and services for the silent auction. Each donor will get up on stage and talk about their prize donation, giving them a chance to also advertise their businesses. It means I'll have to get up on stage and talk about the shop as well.

Eleanor's house is as neat and tidy as the last time I was here, when Jared and I questioned her about the Castle Cove Bandit. It feels like a lifetime ago.

Her bathroom is organized with colored bins hanging on the wall for different products, one color for hand towels, one color for regular towels, and another for loofahs. There's a metal file box attached to the side of the sink for hair dryers and curlers and plant pots that have been repurposed to hold makeup brushes.

Tabby gazes around the room in wonder when we walk in. "It's like a Pinterest mom threw up in here."

"I don't see anything wrong with that," Eleanor says.

"You wouldn't. What are you wearing? Show me, show me."

When Eleanor pulls out a long-sleeved black velvet dress, Tabby makes a face. "Who died and made you buy this?"

"What do you mean? This is elegant." Eleanor holds it up against her body and faces me. "What do you think, Ruby?"

"I think it is very elegant . . . for a funeral."

"See?" Tabby pulls it away and tosses it on the bed. "Don't you have anything else?"

We spend way too much time going through Eleanor's closet.

"Everything you own is black or gray. Are you depressed?" Tabby throws yet another black dress down onto the bed.

"I like dark clothes. They make you look slim, plus they don't stain," Eleanor says.

"Ugh. You are the worst. Wait, what's this?" From the very back recesses of the closet, Tabby pulls out a dark blue dress. The top is a tank-style V-neck and the bottom is a fluffy, sparkly skirt that falls just above the knee.

"Why wouldn't you wear this?" Tabby shakes the garment in Eleanor's direction.

Eleanor bites her lip. "I forgot I had it. I bought it years ago and I've never worn it."

"This is what you are wearing. It's dark, but not 'I think someone might die today' dark." She presses it into Eleanor's arms. "Try it on. I'll start on Ruby's makeup."

We go into the bathroom while Eleanor gets changed and Tabby works on my eye shadow, chattering the whole time about the gala and Ben and how she really needs to get Eleanor to redo her wardrobe to be less school marmish.

It's hard for me to focus because I keep thinking about what's going to happen at the end of the night.

Will Tabby hate me when the truth comes out?

Eleanor comes back into the bathroom with the dress on and Tabby squeals. "Dude. You look hot."

"Troy is going to love you in that," I add from my position on the stool in front of the mirror.

"We're not thinking about that." Tabby grimaces. "But yes, you're hot like a curry."

We spend the next couple of hours doing each other's makeup and hair and Tabby and I get our dresses on.

She's wearing a deep-pink strapless number with sparkly white heels. I opt for a simple black sheath dress. Black seems appropriate for this occasion, since someone will be dying tonight. By tomorrow, the Ruby everyone knows and loves will no longer exist.

When we're all ready and standing together in front of the mirror, admiring our reflections with Tabby in the middle, she links her arms with both of us.

"We are some hot bitches."

~*~

The country club is decked out a lot more than the senior center was for mocktail night, which was the last time we got dressed up in all our finery.

Instead of chintzy streamers and a disco ball, there's a string quartet playing classical music and tables covered in thick, white tablecloths. Fine china and champagne glasses make the room sparkle. It almost looks like a wedding.

I should probably enjoy it as much as I can since I won't ever be having a wedding of my own. At least not with the one person I would want to experience such a thing with. Not that I want to get married right now or anything, I mean, I'm only twenty-one. But still. Any hope of a future with Jared will be ruined after tonight. And rightly so.

There is a dance floor, much bigger and made of what looks like real wood instead of linoleum.

Fortunately, there's not much prep work to do. Everything has been handled quite well by the parents, who are dressed in their finest—Father in a dark, three-piece suit, Mother in a black dress that looks alarmingly like my own.

Figures.

After initial greetings, I avoid the parents as much as I can by helping Eleanor and Tabby sort through the order of announcements for each donation. We have the list of donors, and after dinner and dancing, Tabby will present each prize, give the donor a chance to talk about their business, and then announce the winner for each auction item. Tables set up in the back of the room hold clipboards for people to write their competing bids.

After dinner, Eleanor has made me responsible for watching the bidding tables to help if anyone has questions and to close out the bidding when auctioning is done. Plus to make sure no one cheats. With this crowd, you just never know. Although Tabby's usually the cheater, so since she's helping organize, we might be safe.

The items being offered up for auction vary from dinner for two at the Castle Cove Restaurant to salsa lessons with Mrs. Olsen. There's a free surfing lesson at the pier, a free reading from Ruby (a.k.a. me), a free night's stay at The Seaside Inn, and a free round of golf from the country club, amongst others.

The room fills up quickly with mostly elderly people, all in their sequined and shoulder-padded glory.

Mrs. Olsen has a new cat dress. Unlike the one she wore on mocktail night, this one has a sparkly cat on her chest, not on her butt. How many sequined cat dresses can there possibly be on this planet? Does she commission them?

I mingle with the crowd, making a point of avoiding the parents as I move through the room. I can't avoid them forever. There are only a couple hours until my deadline and possible exposure. I have no more delaying tactics. Just give them what they want. Tell Jared. Focus on the plan.

I talk to Judge Ramsey and his wife for a minute, then listen to Mrs. Hale talk about her newest cake recipe, and even stand next to a sleeping Miss Viola—who probably isn't really sleeping—just to bide my time.

But time is moving faster than a bullet heading straight for my heart. Before I know it, we're all sitting down to eat at a large circular table, Jared, Tabby, Ben, Eleanor, Troy, the parents, and Mrs. Olsen.

Dinner is catered by Castle Cove Restaurant. I make sure to stay away from the fish.

Watching the parents smile and charm everyone at the table makes me want to gouge my own eyes out with a salad fork, but I manage to restrain myself.

If it weren't for the parents' presence, it would be a great night. Jared is the same solicitous, affectionate, considerate date he always is, ratcheting up my guilt from steamy to boiling.

I do love him, even if I haven't said so in so many words, and the realization makes my chest hurt.

After dinner, the string quartet leaves and a different, more lively band sets up. They sing various songs from slow eighties classics to current top forty hits.

I can't enjoy the dancing yet because it's my turn at the bidding tables. I spend an hour answering questions and keeping an eye on the clipboards while watching everyone dancing and enjoying themselves.

Tabby and Ben are scandalizing Mrs. Olsen by dancing way too close. She dances up to them with Mr. Godfrey and smacks Tabby on the arm with her matching sequined cat clutch. She and Tabby start arguing.

I chuckle.

Troy leads Eleanor in a bunch of tango-type moves, which doesn't exactly jive with the Chuck Berry music that's playing, but it is entertaining.

And then there's Jared. Dancing with Mother.

My stomach turns and I look away.

At the opposite end of the room, a figure stands in a shadowed alcove. I can't make out features from where I'm standing, but whoever it is has dark hair and a dark suit. All of the younger people are on the dance floor, so who is it?

The mystery man moves out from the alcove and then down an adjoining hall. I only get a glimpse of his face, but it's familiar. I can't quite place where I've seen him, though . . .

"Hey!" Eleanor pops up in front of me. "I'm here to relieve you."

"Oh, hey, great. Thank you."

"No, thank you for helping. You should go dance with Jared. He's been sulking for the last hour." She winks at me as we pass each other.

Where have I seen that guy before? I always remember faces.

I try to shove thoughts of the mystery man away so I can enjoy these last moments in Jared's arms. Nine o'clock is now less than an hour away.

But my thoughts keep spinning. Even Jared can't keep them away. I hope this works out. I'm counting on the fact that they can't leave town until this farce is over, that they won't be able to access Jared's funds at least until morning.

The music ends and the dancers all halt as Tabby gets up on stage.

"Hey, everyone! The silent auction winners are about to be announced!" There's a smattering of applause from around the room.

"First, the people who donated their prizes are going to come up and talk about their donation and any other goods or services they offer. Then we'll announce the winners. If your name is called, head to the table in the back where our good friend Deputy Reeves will be collecting the money."

Jared gives me one last squeeze around the waist and kisses my head before heading to his post near the back.

The auction begins.

The first prize is from Tabby's hardware store, so she kicks it off by describing the store and what it sells. Her prize is a steep discount on supplies and a consultation for any home remodel or improvement project. I can't help but remember her up on Ruby's roof, tool belt strapped around her waist, patching a stranger's roof. *That's what friends are for*, she said. Whoever wins her prize will be in kind, skilled hands. I shut my eyes and take a deep breath. I can't think about that now.

Once she's done announcing the winner, a name I don't recognize, she moves on to the next donor, some kind of wedding planner.

Another shot to my heart.

I phase out, glancing at the clock and scanning the crowd. My mind buzzing, my stomach already churning with thoughts of how this night will end. How Jared will react. What's going to happen?

Mother stops next to me. "You have thirty minutes."

"I know."

"Meet me out front by the fountain and don't be late or this folder will find it's way into your boyfriend's hands."

She has the folder they brought to the shop the other day, the one with all the evidence against me.

I nod and she disappears.

Shutting my eyes for a moment, I take a deep breath. I can do this.

And then the face of the unknown man flashes in my head, and suddenly I remember.

It's him.

The big-shot attorney my parents were friends with. The one that Paige served drinks to.

Why is he here? Is that who my parents need the money for? Is he here to collect Jared's account numbers, and not them? Are they just the middlemen?

Tabby announces the next silent auction winner, everyone claps, and the crowd shifts, making room for the winner to walk to the back to pay up and collect their certificate. The crowd around me shuffles and parts, and I catch a glimpse of yet another familiar face across the room.

It's not the big-shot attorney.

It's Jackson Murphy.

CHAPTER
TWENTY-ONE

Jackson Murphy is here. Ruby's accountant. The one I keep blowing off because I keep forgetting he exists. Not that I can blame myself, he's way less scary than the parents and not worth nearly as much time and energy . . . unless he were to show up at an inopportune moment. Like now. I only see him for a second, a glimpse of his features between the shifting crowds.

I stretch up on my toes, scanning faces, searching, searching. Where is he going? He heads to the back of the room.

He stops. Next to Jared.

He's talking to Jared.

What is he saying?

I glance over at the clock. It's eight forty-five. I only have fifteen minutes until the parents make good on their promise.

And they're going to give my intel to the big-shot attorney guy. I can't possibly turn it over now. If they have this guy in on their scam, he could run off with Jared's money before I have a chance to tell him the truth.

What do I do?

"Our next prize is a reading from our one and only resident psychic. Ruby, get up here," Tabby calls into the microphone. The spotlight swings in my direction, unerringly finding me in the mass of bodies.

I can't run. I can't hide.

It's too late.

Heart thumping over the cheering of the people around me, I move through the parting crowd up to the stage at the front of the room.

I stand next to Tabby, keeping a smile on my face while my eyes scan the audience and the applause fades out.

The light is too bright. My racing pulse is too loud.

What is Jackson saying to Jared? Will he know everything before I have a chance to confess it all?

Tabby is reading something off a notecard. "Ruby's Readings and Cosmic Shop is more than just your run of the mill new age store—"

"Wait." I step in front of her, cutting her off and speaking into her microphone. "I have to tell you something."

I glance uneasily back at Tabby before turning to face the crowd.

I can't make out individual faces under the glare of the lights, just blobs of dark, shifting figures. I take a deep, steadying breath. The adrenaline racing through my veins makes me both shaky and alert.

I have to do this. Now.

They're all going to hate me.

But I can't turn back.

Keep Paige safe.

"I'm not Ruby." Feedback distorts the last word.

Miss Viola pipes up, way too loud. "Did she say booby?"

"Um." Tabby laughs, the sound a bit strangled. She steps to my side, using one hand to shade her eyes from the spotlight. "No, Miss Viola. She said she's not Ruby."

She turns her confused gaze in my direction.

"Of course you're Ruby." She gestures toward me, her brow furrowed. She covers the mic with one hand. "Are you drunk?"

"No, I'm not. I'm not drunk and I'm not Ruby." My voice is shaking. I nudge her hand off the mic, clear my throat, and try to breathe. I have to get this out. "The truth is, I've been lying."

The words leave my mouth, as does the crushing weight on my shoulders. No more trying to hide the truth. "I've lied to all of you. I didn't mean to. It just happened."

The pervasive silence in the room speaks volumes. No one is moving. No one is saying a word.

I can't stop now. I have to finish this, finish everything.

"The real Ruby left for India months ago. She was here less than a day. She hired me to look after her shop and . . . but then this girl showed up asking for a reading and we had no money. I shouldn't have done it. I knew it was wrong. But I didn't know what else to do. So I lied. To all of you. "

I swallow even though my mouth is as dry as the sand on Castle Cove beach at low tide. But just like the tide, the words are coming faster now, unstoppable, rushing in to fill the silence.

"I pretended to be Ruby. I thought it would only be the one time, but then there was the mugging and Jared," I gesture in his direction, even though I can't see him, "and—and I have no excuses for what I've done. But I had to tell you all now, because the truth about what's happening here tonight, this *charity*," the word tastes foul in my mouth, "is more important than my lies. Out of everything I've done and said, I regret more than anything coming to Castle Cove, because that brought the Hamptons here, too. You see, that's not their real name and they don't run any kind of charitable organization. The reason Paige and I came here in the first place was to get away from them. They're con artists and swindlers, and it's my fault they came here and took your money for this farce. There is no charity. Your money will be going to line their pockets."

There's a collective gasp from the crowd.

"This is better than my stories on the TV," Mrs. Olsen stage-whispers from somewhere near the front.

More gasps, startled murmurs, people shifting and glancing around.

There's a slow clap from somewhere in the crowd.

The bodies shift out of the way. I put a hand up to try and block the bright stage light.

Father.

"It's a nice story, but it's obvious this is just more lies. Why should anyone believe you?" His voice booms out over the crowd, strong and full of conviction. "You've already admitted to lying and stealing their money long before we arrived. Now you're trying to blame us to get the attention off of you. We aren't the con artists here," he says.

All eyes swing in my direction.

"I'm not lying," I say. "Well, I was . . . I mean, I'm not any longer."

This is ridiculous. *I* barely even believe me.

There's a loud shout near the front door and the crowd turns again. Murmurs begin building in the back of the room.

I brace myself for what's coming. It doesn't matter. Even though it does. I can't see anyone in the crowd anyway, no point in looking there. Besides, Tabby is staring at me, curiosity and uncertainty warring in her expression.

But I don't have time to say anything else.

The crowd is shifting and restless, the voices rising in the small space, and then someone jumps up on stage.

It's Jared, in his tux, his hair a bit ruffled. His eyes are bright and his jaw is clenched. "I'm afraid I have to take you in."

CHAPTER TWENTY-TWO

"You can't arrest her." Tabby's voice echoes over the microphone, above the crowd's growing hum.

She's watching us, her eyes wide and shocked.

My heart both fills and hurts. She's still defending me.

But I have to go with him.

"Stay out of it, Tabby." Jared takes my arm and pulls me off the stage.

We go through the back behind the curtain, away from the anxious audience.

We're in a back hallway when Tabby catches up with us. "You have to tell me what's going on."

"You shouldn't defend me. I've been lying to you this whole time."

"No you haven't."

Frustrated, I come to a sudden stop, halting Jared's forward progress.

I swallow and look her in the eyes. "I have." She deserves the truth. "I'm not a good person."

She's stunned into silence, something I've never seen before.

I jerk out of Jared's grasp. "I'm not going to run. You don't have to hold me." I keep walking in the direction we were going, Jared keeping pace behind me.

I don't look back.

In the parking lot, I follow him to his Jeep. He opens the passenger door for me. The ride to the station is tense and silent. I want to ask him what's going on, what he's thinking, but I don't. I can't look at him. I don't want to see how much I've hurt him.

Once at the station, I'm cuffed and taken into a small interrogation room, and still without saying a word, he leaves.

I don't know how long I'm left there, but it feels like at least an hour.

Long enough for me to replay the scene from the gala in my mind, the words Father shouted, the evidence they surely have against me.

But I have a little hope. Even if I'm locked away, I can tell them about Paige and make sure she's safe and away from them.

When the door opens, it's Jared again.

He's still dressed in his tuxedo from the gala, but it's significantly more rumpled since the last time I saw it. His tie is hanging around his neck and the top buttons of his shirt are undone. His hair looks as though he's been running his hands through it. It's the least put together I've ever seen him, but his eyes find mine unerringly.

They aren't the same eyes that have been watching me for the past three weeks. Not the eyes full of laughter, shared jokes, and comfort. His gaze is as enigmatic and inscrutable as when we first met, when I was sure he hated me, when I couldn't tell what he was thinking.

We stare at each other in silence, eyeing each other up.

I have no idea what to say. His eyes continue to search mine, as if seeking the truth, but I don't know what truth he needs.

I wasn't expecting him.

I thought once he discovered the truth, at best he would leave me to my fate. Have one of the other officers interrogate and book me. Ignore me completely like he did on the drive over. It's what I deserve. I don't deserve his regard or even his anger.

He doesn't say anything. He enters the room, leaving the door open behind him. But he doesn't come in any farther, lingering near the exit instead.

I stand but I don't know why. Where am I going to go?

"Hi," I say. Brilliant.

"Hi," he repeats. "What's your real name?"

I swallow past the lump in my throat. "Charlotte." Finally. *My* name. I'll never have to hear him call me Ruby again. Well, more than likely I won't hear him call me anything again. But still, the relief is acute.

He nods. "Can I get you anything to drink?"

I sigh and slump back down in my chair. So this is what we've been reduced to. Cops and robbers.

He's here to act like he cares so I'll open up and confess to everything.

I could say yes, ask for food to go with the drink, drag it out and see if I can get any information or anything out of them in return. Cut a deal. But I'm not that person anymore.

"Why don't we dispense with the interrogation tactics and you just tell me what you want from me?"

He doesn't say anything for a few long seconds. Then he shuts the door softly and sits in front of me. He pulls his little black notebook out of his pocket, the same one he used when we worked together on the Castle Cove Bandit. "Information."

"What kind of information?"

"How much do you know about the Hamptons?"

I smile, even though I don't feel like it. The motion is reflexive. This is what I wanted—to come clean. But at the same time, I know the truth is going to hurt. Me. Him. It's all the same thing. "First of all, they aren't really the Hamptons. That's a fake name."

There's no hint of surprise. He already knows. Interesting.

How much does he know? About them, and about me? Obviously not enough if the need for information is there.

"What are their real names?"

"I'm not sure. They never told me."

His brows furrow. "You don't know your own aunt's and uncle's names?"

I chuckle a bit. "They aren't my aunt and uncle. They're my parents."

His expression doesn't change but he rocks back in his seat a couple inches.

I've surprised him. So this much he didn't know.

"How can you not know your parents' names?"

"Trust me, that's not even close to the strangest part of my childhood. You want to hear about it?"

He nods, the movement quick and small.

And then I open my mouth, and out comes the truth. About my childhood. About Paige. I don't tell him everything I know about Paige, yet. Just about how I raised my little sister amongst thieves and scoundrels, about how we eventually had to escape.

At first, I try to be brave and watch him while I tell the story, but I can't. My eyes stray to the table in front of me and stay fixed there. On my own hands, which are clasped together.

"I didn't mean to be Ruby. We were running out of money, and this girl came to the shop asking for a reading. She offered me two hundred dollars. I just . . ." I shrug helplessly. "I took the opportunity that presented itself. But then she was robbed. And you came to the door."

"And you kept up the pretense that you were Ruby."

"I didn't see another way out."

"You could have told me the truth."

"I didn't know that. I didn't know you. My whole life I've learned to trust no one. Especially cops. All I've known is lies and deceit. I'm not a good person."

The truth is almost freeing.

The words keep tumbling out. I tell him everything. How we set up the cameras around town to get intel, how I used him when we were investigating the break-ins to see if the parents were involved. Then probably the worst part, how I stole the jewelry from Pearl to try and frame the parents, how it got turned around on me, setting it up for Jared to find the jewelry.

He doesn't seem terribly surprised to learn I'm the Castle Cove Ninja. "That night . . . you were using me then, too?"

"Not using you." How can I make him understand? "I tried to protect you. I told you I'm no good for anyone. I didn't want to hurt you. Or Tabby or anyone else. But I did. I shouldn't have let anyone get so close. And then the parents were here and they wanted to run a real con, not the small potatoes I've been running. I wanted to take Paige and run, but they took our car and our money. They wanted to take Paige too but they told me they would sign her over to me and disappear if I helped them. I bugged the shop, I trailed them around town, I framed them for robbery, I stalled, stalled, *stalled*. But nothing worked. I even—"

I look up into the harsh fluorescent lights above us, not letting the tears escape. I have to tell him this part.

"I hacked into one of your bank accounts. Once they realized you had significant assets, they wanted to steal from you, too. I didn't want to do it, but I gave them one of your account numbers. A small one. It was just to stall them, put them off until I could take them down."

His brows are drawn together but he's otherwise blank as he watches me for a few, long moments. I expected an outburst. Some yelling or pacing or slamming of doors. Instead, he surprises me.

"Where's Paige?"

I swallow. "I kept her safe. She's okay."

"I'm sure she is, but we need to know where she is." His eyes aren't so hard anymore. They've softened a bit.

Does he believe me? Does he blame me? He should.

Especially if he believes me.

"I don't . . . I can't tell you unless you promise you won't give her to them. They aren't good people. I . . ."

And now I have to give him the full truth. My last card. "There's another reason you can't let them have her. Paige isn't their real daughter." It almost hurts to admit the truth out loud. Paige isn't really my sister. Except, she is.

His eyes sharpen. "Why do you say that?"

"They have some documents locked in a safe. I broke into it—"

"With the neodymium magnet you stole from the station?" he interjects.

I nod, watching him closely. I can't tell if he totally hates me now or not. His expression is unreadable. "There's a birth certificate with the name Andrea Winchester. Same age as Paige. Parents were Mary and John. I did some research and found an article from the year Paige—*Andrea* was born. Her parents died and left her a bunch of money in a trust. She was kidnapped when she was only a couple months old. I think my parents are the ones who took her."

I tell him about the attorney guy, the way my parents had Paige bring him and his cronies their drinks. How unusual it was. How he was there tonight at the gala and how the parents must be working with him or owe him something.

Finally, I tell him where I took Paige. To Camp Umpqua up in the mountains, with Naomi. The parents would never think to look for her there, plus she's surrounded by other kids and counselors. I gave the head counselor a giant sob story about how our parents had died suddenly—that was pure wish fulfillment—and Paige needed to spend some time at camp as a distraction. I promised to pay them when I came to pick Paige up. I *might* have also dropped Jared's name to get them to believe me. It worked like a charm.

He doesn't say anything, just nods at the information and makes a note in his book.

Frustration at his lack of expression bubbles inside me.

"I know I've broken like a hundred laws. You can put me away. I just want Paige to be taken care of. And away from them. I'll testify, I'll go to prison, I'll do whatever you want if you keep her safe. You promised me before." My voice cracks a little on the last word. I've talked so much my throat is dry.

Still, he doesn't respond. Instead, he stands and leaves the room. I don't know whether to cry or laugh or bash my head against the table. But I don't have to wait long for him to return. Less than a minute later, he comes back into the room and hands me a bottle of water.

When I try to open it with my cuffed hands, he makes a small, frustrated noise and then removes the cuffs.

His hands don't linger on mine. Every movement is quick, efficient, and impersonal. And with each detached motion, something strong and sharp stabs my chest.

I gather myself and my emotions—they won't save me or Paige now—and gulp down a few swallows of the cold water before asking, "What's going to happen now?"

His mouth flattens into a thin line.

I can't tell if he's irritated with me or the situation in general or with something else happening beyond this room.

"I can't tell you yet. But I have one more question."

"Shoot."

"Why didn't you just turn your parents in when they first came to town?"

"To who? Who would believe me? They'd already set the trap of being my aunt and uncle. Exposing them would have meant telling the truth about who I really am. I would have had to admit I had lied and deceived, and then ask people to trust that I was telling the truth. I didn't think anyone would believe me."

"But now you do?"

"No, I don't. But what happens to me doesn't matter anymore. I thought I could fix everything without help." I slump back in the seat with a sigh, shutting my eyes for a moment before opening them again and looking up at him. "But once I learned the truth about Paige, none of that mattered anymore. I knew I had a way to protect her, regardless of what happened to me. You don't have to believe me. You can confirm the truth about Paige, and then you can protect her. That's all I want."

He watches me closely and then nods, as if I've just confirmed something he already suspected. "We have a bed ready for you, so you can get some sleep." His voice is brusque and businesslike. Like I'm just one more criminal he has to deal with at work.

"Here?"

He nods.

I'm too exhausted to argue, and the truth is, I don't want to be released. All that awaits me beyond these walls are people I've scammed and the parents.

I follow him without argument down the empty hall and past rows of vacant cells with barren bed frames and layers of dust. He leads me to the open door of the last stall at the very end. It's been swept out and there are clean sheets on the cot, along with what looks like a brand new pillow. Folded clothes sit on top of a chair in the corner.

There's even a bag of takeout that I can smell from the doorway. I know what it is without looking. It's my favorite meal from Stella's: a cheeseburger and fries. A last meal?

I pause before going in. Being locked into a small room does not sound enticing, even with all the amenities.

"If you aren't charging me with anything, you can't keep me here."

"I know."

I hesitate, only for a second, and then step into the cell.

He backs up, leaving.

"Wait." I swallow, my tongue thick in my dry mouth. "Paige . . ."

His voice is quiet when he responds. "She's going to be okay. And you are, too. I can't tell you anything else right now. But I promise it will all end up okay. Do you trust me?"

The question he's been asking me, and I've been asking myself, for the last three months. I finally have a real answer. "Yes."

Then he leaves, the door to the cell sliding shut behind him with a decisive click.

And then I'm alone. There's one high-set, narrow window facing the front parking lot. I have to get up on my tiptoes to look out of it. Two black sedans and an empty police cruiser sit out front. The sky is brightening in the distance. The sun will be rising soon.

I'm exhausted.

I make quick work of the food. Someone also left a new bar of soap next to the sink and I use it to clean up as much as I can. I'm surprised to find the clothes on the chair are mine. Someone got them from my house. I cringe. Ruby's house. My old sweats, a T-shirt, and then a summer dress Tabby gave me. Under the chair is a pair of sandals that were also a gift from Tabby. Why are those here? Who brought them? I'm too tired to try and dissect it all.

I put on the sweats and T-shirt and crawl onto the bed, at first a little grossed out by the thought of sleeping on a jail cell cot, but the sheets smell like dryer sheets and I'm almost too wiped out to care.

What if this doesn't work? What if Jared is so mad at me he doesn't take care of Paige? What if she ends up alone or in foster care or . . . ?

I shut my eyes against the thoughts crowding my brain.

I trust Jared. I know he'll do what's right.

~*~

I've barely shut my eyes when a noise wakes me up. I can't believe I fell asleep at all.

It's the cell door opening.

The sound jars me awake, and I sit up with a start before rubbing my eyes and focusing on my visitor.

It's Anderson.

My heart drops a little that it's not Jared, although I don't know why I would want to see him right now. Don't need to dig the knife in any deeper.

Anderson nods at me. He's wearing his uniform. His expression is somber but his eyes are warm. "I've got to take you to the court room."

"Court room?"

"We have a small arraignment room set up for Judge Ramsey. Haven't used it in almost five years, but it's here."

"Arraignment? What am I being charged with? Jared told me I wasn't being charged with anything."

Anderson shrugs. "I guess identity theft or something. I think they brought up the charges just this morning."

"Can I talk to Jared first?" I haven't even been booked. They can't do this.

"Not yet. He'll be there, though. I'm just supposed to get you ready and take you in. We have twenty minutes. I'll be at the end of the hall. Just holler when you're ready."

I'm not entirely sure what to make of this new development. An arraignment? Jared told me less than eight hours ago that he wasn't charging me. What's changed?

Trust me, he said.

I guess this is one way to test it.

With numb fingers, I put on the dress that was left for me and the sandals.

I pull my hair into a knot in the back of my head as best I can, wash my face and call for Anderson.

When he comes back, he's got a set of handcuffs.

"Just a formality," he assures me when my eyes drop to the silver objects.

I nod and stick my hands out dutifully.

Keeping my head down, I follow him out of the holding area and back into the main building.

I hear the voices before I see them. Some kind of chanting, the words too muffled to discern. But the sound gets louder and louder the closer we get.

We turn down a wide hallway and there they are.

The first person I notice is Tabby. She's leading a line of people, and they're all holding signs. Hers reads *Free Not-Ruby*.

A startled laugh escapes me.

More people with different signs are crowded behind her. Eleanor is holding a sign that says, *What she says*, and it's pointing at Tabby. Mrs. Olsen is in an oversized Garfield shirt with cat-print leggings, her own colorful sign reading *#Resist*. Then there's Miss Viola in her wheelchair, Mr. Bingel and the boys—each with their own signs—and more. It looks like half the town is here.

When they spot me coming down the hall, they go a little crazy, waving, clapping, and cheering.

What are they doing here?

"Are you letting her go?" Tabby demands once we're in earshot.

"Tabby, you know I can't tell you anything about that. Now if you'll get out of the way."

"This is a miscarriage of justice!" she yells. "We demand you release her immediately."

A few hollers of agreement erupt behind her.

He sighs. "Why don't you talk to your brother? He'll explain to you that I have to do this."

"My brother is a moron."

The door to the arraignment room opens, and Troy sticks his head out.

"There's the moron now!" Mrs. Olsen yells.

Troy frowns. "What have I missed?" His eyes meet Anderson's and then flick to mine. "Good, you guys are here. Come on in, we're ready for you." He holds the door open wider.

Tabby yells, "What is happening in there?"

"This isn't a public hearing, Tabby."

"That's bullshit. Our voices will be heard!"

"Just let them in, Troy," Jared calls from inside the room.

Troy rolls his eyes but opens the door a bit wider, and the crowd filters in.

Jared was smart to allow them to enter. Apparently soothed by having one of their demands met, they mellow out a bit, the dissension diminishing into quieter grumbles and whispers, mostly wondering what's going on from the sound of it.

An answer I'm seeking as well.

Anderson and I follow in behind the mob, but Troy moves out into the hallway, shutting the door behind him.

It's set up sort of like a courtroom, with a desk up front for a bench. Facing it is another table and folding chairs for litigants. Jared is sitting at the table on one side, facing the bench, his back to me, but he's dressed in his police uniform. Chairs for the public face the setup, but there aren't enough for the number of people who've barged in. Some stay standing in the back.

Anderson leads me to the seat next to Jared and I sit. I try to catch Jared's eye but he says something to Anderson, leaning close to his ear and keeping his voice low too low to hear. Anderson nods and then heads back to the door. He sticks his head out and relays whatever the message was to Troy.

I don't have time to speak or ask what's going on, because a side door opens and Judge Ramsey walks in. He's not wearing a robe or anything, just a simple gray suit and dark-blue tie.

When he walks in, everyone stands.

"Sit down. This isn't a trial." He motions to everyone before sitting at the table in the front of the room, facing the rest of us. "You want to explain why we are here today, Deputy?"

Jared stands. "We're here to determine if charges should be pressed against this woman, Charlotte . . ." He pauses and finally, finally looks at me. "What's your last name?"

I shrug. I have no idea what my full legal name is.

"Against Charlotte." There's a flicker of something in his eyes. Surprise? Pity? I can't tell because he looks away too quickly.

"We don't know if there are charges to be brought?" Judge Ramsey asks, his brows furrowing, and for a second I get a glimpse of the power behind the wire-framed glasses. His voice, although not loud, holds the authority of someone who's used to being in charge.

"Correct, Your Honor. We asked you here in case anyone has cause to charge Charlotte with a crime."

"This is a bit unconventional, but I trust you will explain all in due course, Deputy." He nods at Jared.

"Yes, Your Honor."

A bit unconventional? That's like saying Satan is a bit evil.

"The first people we brought in to be interviewed are Charlotte's aunt and uncle, David and Leah Hampton," Jared says.

I can't help but note he didn't call them my parents, even though I told him they were actually my parents and that David and Leah aren't their real names. Does he not believe me?

The rear door opens and Anderson lets them in. Murmurs and shuffling fills the room as they come to the front, and then the parents are there, standing between the judge and Jared. Mother has red-rimmed eyes, and she's clutching a handkerchief in one hand. Father looks somber and tired. They are the perfect picture of grieving relatives. Father has a briefcase in one hand.

"Can you tell us what you know about Charlotte?" Jared's voice is gentle.

Does he believe them over me?

"We only ask for leniency for our dear niece." Mother grips the handkerchief tighter and holds it up to her nose. "After her parents passed, she . . . didn't do well with the trauma. The doctors say she has a persecutory delusional disorder. When someone experiences a shock, sometimes their brain has a bit of a break. In her case, it's caused her to believe we are out to get her. It's to be expected, since she was so young, and she's always had a rather fragile constitution. We thought she was getting better, but then we discovered it was getting worse. That's why we had to follow her here to Castle Cove. Paige called us and told us what was going on, and we knew her psychotic break was worse than ever before. She was stealing from people."

I can only stare in shock. This is the angle they want to go for, that I'm crazy?

I can feel the eyes of the people behind me boring into me, and I try to look as sane as possible.

"Stealing?" Jared asks. "Because she pretended to be Ruby?"

Father opens his briefcase and hands him a sheaf of papers. "It was worse than that. We found these in her house when we were trying to find Paige. I think you'll recognize those accounts, Deputy. Charlotte has a problem. She thinks she needs money and she uses people to get it. She's the one who stole the jewels and we have proof."

Jared flips through the papers.

I can't see them from where I am, but I imagine they are the same photographs they showed me before. I'm glad I already told all of these things to Jared.

"Why didn't you say anything to anyone about Charlotte not being Ruby?" Jared asks.

"We didn't want her to get in trouble. It's not her fault. You see, she's suffered from these breakdowns before and she just doesn't know what she's doing. We thought if we played along for a little bit, we could convince her to come back home with us and we could take care of her, no harm done."

"So you're saying she's mentally unstable?"

Mother lets out a brief sob. "Yes."

"But you let her care for her young sister even though you know she has these problems?"

Mother's hand flaps and she dabs her eyes with the cloth in her hand. "We thought she was better. She had been on medication and seeing a therapist for some time. And she's always loved Paige. Her mental disorder doesn't cause her to harm others, at least it never has before. And we let Paige know we were here for her, so if there was ever any trouble, she could come to us."

"Do you know where Paige is now?"

There's a brief flicker in Mother's eyes. "No. And we're so frightened." Now she breaks down in sobs, grasping Father's coat and burying her face in his shoulder.

Brava. I would slow-clap if it wouldn't lend credence to my "persecutory delusions."

Jared thanks the parents and they move back to their seats somewhere behind me, Mother still clutching Father while he consoles her and she sniffs into his neck.

Ugh.

Troy sticks his head in the room and nods in my direction.

No, not my direction, Jared's direction.

Jared flicks a hand at Anderson.

What are they doing?

"So we have potential crimes of kidnapping, impersonation and identity theft, and then this," he holds up the papers the parents provided.

"Fraudulent withdrawal, robbery, fraud, and obstruction of justice. Let's address these one at a time. The first one is impersonation and identity theft. For that, I'd like to introduce everyone to Ruby Simpson. The real Ruby."

Murmurs swell around the room in a wave as Anderson opens the door and Ruby walks in, Jackson Murphy in tow.

She looks the same as when I last saw her, except a bit tanner and blonder, and her hair has grown a little. She's wearing a long skirt and sandals and a tank top with crochet straps.

She waltzes in and smiles warmly at everyone, her face lighting the room. The murmurs swell into loud talk and speculation. Jackson's expression is much more serious. He's wearing a suit and he also has a briefcase. More evidence against me?

They walk to the front of the room and stand between Jared and Judge Ramsey.

I'm not sure what to expect. Is she going to be angry? But then she grins down at me.

"Are you Ruby Simpson?" Jared asks her.

"Yes."

"Did you know this woman was impersonating you?"

"No. Not until this morning, when my accountant and your officer outside there," she motions to the door, "met me at the shop."

"And now that you know, do you intend to press charges?"

"Oh, absolutely not." She puts a hand on her chest. "Charlotte may have been using my name, but she has done a great job with everything during my absence. In fact, the store has done better in her care than it would have in mine, I'm sure. My accountant went through the records this morning and everything is in perfect order. We're already making a profit."

"So it doesn't bother you that she pretended to be you?"

"It's a little odd, I admit. And I can't speak for her giving readings to people or what she's said, but I think she's done more good than harm from what I've been hearing."

"She hasn't done anything wrong," Tabby's voice yells over the crowd. "She's helped everyone here. Real Ruby is right."

"She saved my life," Miss Viola says. "Sort of."

"She saved us, too." Little Gary and Greg step forward with Mr. Bingel behind them.

"And in doing so, she saved me, too," says Mr. Bingel.

A chorus of voices rises, chiming in.

"She helped me get rid of the little people!"

"She listened to me when no one else would!"

"She's the reason I'm baking again!"

"I don't know why I'm here!"

"Okay everyone, quiet!" bellows Jared. The crowd simmers down and shifts uncomfortably in their seats. "We're not saying Ruby, I mean Charlotte, isn't a good person. What we're trying to do here is follow the law, and there are still some things that need to be resolved. Now, her family is saying she might be a danger to herself and others because of a mental condition and that she kidnapped a minor child. Those are serious charges. We can't just let them slide."

"It's just her word against theirs," Tabby calls out. "How do we know they aren't lying?"

I would kiss her right now if I weren't handcuffed and she weren't across the room.

"There's really only one way to know. We have to ask Paige," Jared says.

The door in the back opens again and this time Paige walks in. She's flanked by two people in suits. Two people I recognize. The couple that was at the shop the other day, the ones acting a bit off right before the parents came in with their ultimatum.

"Come on up here, Paige," Jared calls out.

Paige winks as she walks by.

She knows something.

"Why don't you tell us your side of the story, honey," Judge Ramsey says.

She bites her lip and glances around. "Charlotte isn't crazy. Yes, she pretended to be Ruby, but it was only so we could have some money for food and stuff. It was more my fault than hers."

"It wasn't your fault," I speak for the first time. "I take full responsibility for everything."

"You can't say you kidnapped me, not when I came with you willingly." Her eyes leave mine to flick to Jared and then to Judge Ramsey. "They aren't our aunt and uncle. They're our parents."

A gasp goes through the crowd.

Paige is still talking. "They aren't nice people. You guys don't understand. We had to leave. Charlotte wanted me to have a normal life. I was never allowed to go to school. They barely let me leave the house unless it was for a con."

She stops talking and looks at me.

It feels like everyone in the room is watching me, waiting.

"Our parents are con artists," I say. "I knew how to pretend to be Ruby because that's the life I've lived. I wanted to protect Paige from that. But it didn't work. I can't protect her. And I *should* be charged with a crime. I lied to all of you. You can send me away, just please, please take care of Paige. She's innocent in all of this."

"No one can take her, she's our daughter!" Mother yells.

"Now that, we know, is not true." Jared slips opens the file on the table. "She's not your daughter. I have her birth certificate." He waves it in the air. "She's the daughter of John and Mary Winchester, who are both deceased. I have the proof here."

The whole room explodes.

Judge Ramsey bangs on the table until the voices quiet down.

Jared continues. "Paige's real name is Andrea. Her parents died in a plane crash when she was just an infant, and these people kidnapped her."

"That's a lie!" Father shouts.

"It's not." The stocky guy in the suit with Paige speaks up.

The parents recognize the tables have turned. They rush for the exit, but the room is too small for them to slip out unnoticed.

"Someone stop them," Jared calls out.

There are too many people here against them now. Mrs. Olsen pushes Miss Viola's wheelchair, tripping Father, and the two suits are on him. Anderson grabs Mother, and the suits click handcuffs on the duo with ease.

Mother's face is ashen and Father's jaw is clenched. It's the last thing I see before they're escorted out of the room.

I whip back toward Jared. That couple. They came into the shop that day, acting strange. And there was the nondescript sedan, the one I thought was following us after our day at the beach. The same one that drove by when I was casing the parents' house. The clothes, the haircuts, the way they move like they're in charge of everything. They must be FBI, or some kind of federal agents. They've been here, in town for a while. Have they been working with the local PD? Has Jared known about them, about everything this whole time?

Paige runs into me, throwing her arms around my waist. My hands are still cuffed, so all I can do is lean my head against hers.

"What does this mean?" I ask Jared, my eyes meeting his over Paige's head.

"It means we used this fake arraignment to get your parents here in front of witnesses. It means we aren't going to be charging you with anything but . . ."

His eyes flick behind me.

One of the suits is back. The woman. She makes her way up to the front of the room where we're standing. "I'm Agent Sparks. I'm afraid you'll have to come with me."

They're taking me, too.

"No!" Paige says, her arms holding me a little tighter.

I nod at the agent, my throat full of emotion. "Can you just give me a second?" I turn back to Jared. "What about Paige?"

"She'll be okay," he says quietly, and then without removing his eyes from mine, he pulls another stack of papers from his file. "Your Honor, while you're here, I was wondering if you would sign some temporary guardianship papers until we can contact the relatives of Andrea Winchester."

He walks to Judge Ramsey.

"I had someone at the county draw these up this morning so she can live with me, since she has stayed with me before."

Judge Ramsey lifts a brow. "If there are no objections?"

No one objects. The people in the room are too busy murmuring to one another, reiterating the story, watching me and Paige. Or Andrea. I don't know if I can get used to her real name.

"Paige, you can go with him. It's going to be okay."

Her head shakes back and forth against my chest. "No."

Jared walks over to us, leans down, and whispers something in Paige's ear. I can't hear the words because suddenly Tabby is there, questioning Agent Sparks.

"Where are you taking her? Are you charging her with something? She didn't do anything wrong!"

"Ma'am, I'm going to have to ask you to step back, please." Agent Sparks's voice is clear and strong and no-nonsense.

"You aren't the boss of me."

"Tabby." Troy comes up behind her. "You have to get out of the way."

"I do what I want!"

With an apologetic look at Agent Sparks, Troy picks Tabby up, slinging her over his shoulder.

"This is anarchy!" she yells as she's carted out of the room.

I just shake my head and laugh, but it emerges as more of a sob.

Agent Sparks faces me. "Am I going to have to carry you out of here, too?"

"No. I'm ready." And with one last glance at Jared and Paige, I turn and follow her out of the room.

CHAPTER TWENTY-THREE

I spend the next four days in a small FBI office in Portland.

I talk to psychologists and various agents who all start to look the same, reiterating my story over and over and over. They're especially interested in the hot-shot attorney guy. I find out his name is Bradford Stone. Apparently, the parents tried to run a con on him, but it backfired and then he was blackmailing them for money and/or Paige, who they couldn't give up because they needed her for their trust-fund scam.

"They really thought Paige would turn eighteen and just hand over the money?" I ask Agent Sparks.

She shrugs. "Maybe they hoped to ransom her. Or blackmail her."

Hanging with the feds is actually not too bad. Agent Sparks is fairly young, only twenty-eight, and she's nicer than I imagined an FBI agent would be to a young con like me. After the first day, we almost come to some sort of understanding of one another. I wouldn't say we're friends, she's not like Tabby, but we get along.

She stays in a hotel with me, adjoining rooms, and we get room service every night. Every day I tell her, everyone else at the small office, and more people via conference and video call everything I know about everything that happened in Castle Cove. I even tell them about my childhood and young adult life. Over and over again. Then there's paperwork that has to be signed, statements, you name it.

On the third day, I see Bradford Stone. They bring him in and I have to ID him as the man I saw with my parents the night they made Paige act as a cocktail waitress. Also the same person I saw loitering around the gala the other night.

"You have a good memory for details," Agent Sparks tells me. "And it's impressive how you pieced information together."

I shrug. "I've adapted."

Once they have gathered enough information and done their own research and hacking, they have enough evidence to nail the parents. For good. Or for at least twenty years in a federal penitentiary. They don't tell me all the details, but I pick up enough.

I even learn their real names: Donna and Alan Crowley.

And just like that, I have a last name. Charlotte Crowley. Once I'm alone, I repeat the name out loud a few times, the syllables foreign and awkward against my tongue. I'm not sure what I had hoped for, exactly, but even saying the name over and over doesn't lend me any sense of possession. More like they belong to someone else, some other Charlotte.

As for the parents, they have such innocuous names. Donna and Alan. Not that I really expected them to be named Beelzebub and Medusa, but I expected something a little less . . . normal.

"Do you want to talk to your parents before we're done with all this?" Agent Sparks keeps asking me.

No, I don't want to see them. Ever.

Agent Sparks shares information with me when we're at the hotel and away from the office. She can't tell me everything, but she probably discloses more than she should.

Father was raised as a con artist, just like me. But his parents were charged and imprisoned when he was fourteen. He was sent to live with an uncle who used him as a drug runner. When the uncle also went to prison, Father was tossed around from foster home to foster home before finally aging out of the system and starting up his own rackets.

Agent Sparks thinks it's rather amazing he didn't get caught himself, or turn into some kind of druggie. Most do, apparently. Her eyes are sad when she tells me that, and it makes me wonder about the things she has to deal with on a daily basis.

He met Mother when he was running a con on her parents. This part I already knew, but Agent

Sparks adds some details that put the old story in a new light.

It's true that Mother was raised by a wealthy family, but it sounds as though they were just as crooked as Father's, albeit in a more white-collar way. Her father was a banker who allegedly laundered money for the mafia, and she was raised by a string of nannies. When Father and Mother first met, they had an instant connection. They understood each other, despite his more rugged upbringing. She helped him con her parents and then they ran away together. They've been running ever since.

I was an accident. I knew that. I am their biological daughter, but they didn't want children.

Then came Paige. Or, really, Andrea.

Mother was already pretending to be pregnant for a con when they saw the article about Andrea's parents in the paper. It was perfect. They took her and pretended she was theirs. After all, who would suspect them when she'd had a pregnant belly for months? They moved so much anyway, we left the area before Paige was more than six months old. It explains why they kept her relatively secluded. They raised her as their own, treating her better than they did me.

"Why is that?" I wonder aloud.

"Andrea was their ticket to wealth. Their retirement plan, so to speak. Plus, they may have some degree of self-hatred. Maybe they projected those feelings onto you, while Andrea, who doesn't carry their DNA, embodies something better. A better life. A kinder world."

Agent Sparks also explains a few other pieces I had been wondering about. Namely, Ruby. When Jackson Murphy, the accountant, had been trying to reach me, it was to let me know that she was coming back early. Apparently, her time with the Maharishi was cut short when he had to leave for speaking engagements on some kind of world tour.

Anyway, the whole FBI debriefing thing isn't bad, especially since it becomes clear fairly quickly that they aren't throwing the book at me. But I miss Paige. And Jared.

And Tabby, but that doesn't last as long.

I only have one more day left in Portland. Agent Sparks and I are sitting on the couch in my hotel room, watching reruns of *The Andy Griffith Show* and eating room service, when there's a knock at the door.

We look at each other. "Did you order any more food?" she asks.

"No."

She gets up to check it out. Her hand unsnaps the gun always at her side, but she doesn't pull it out of the holster. Looking through the keyhole, she releases a muttered curse.

She opens the door, but I can't see beyond her frame. "I've told you at least twenty times to leave me alone. How did you find us?"

"What? Like it was supposed to be hard?" I recognize the voice. "You told me that once you caught the bad guy I could see her. Well you caught him. And here I am."

It's true, Agent Sparks told me that just today Bradford Stone was taken into federal custody. But there's been no press release. The FBI hasn't had a chance to throw one together yet.

"How did you—" Agent Sparks throws up her hands and moves back as Tabby shoves through the doorway. "Your friend is remarkably persistent. I'll be next door if you need me."

She disappears back into the adjoining room, leaving the door open an inch.

Tabby is here. She's *here*. She's wearing the same colorful top and jeans she had on when I first met her, except this time, instead of holding a casserole and standing on Ruby's porch, she's hovering near the door, as determined as I've ever seen her.

"Tabby what are you—"

"Do you know how hard it is to get an FBI agent to crack? It's like trying to nail jelly to a tree."

I laugh and some of my tension eases. She must not hate me. She's here, she's making jokes. No matter what else I've lost, if I still have a friend, that's . . . everything. "But you managed it."

She smiles. "You're damn right I did." She still hasn't moved away from the entryway.

I clasp my hands together in front of me and meet her eyes. "I'm so sorry. You're the only friend I've ever had, and I lied to you. You have every right to hate me."

"I don't hate you." She finally walks into the room and plops on the couch, right next to where I'm still standing. "I'll forgive you, but only if you spill it all. And give me the rest of your fries. And any time we play games, you have to let me win."

Laughing, I sit next to her. "Is that it?"

"And you have to name your first child after me."

"Even if it's a boy?"

Her lips purse and her eyes narrow at me. "Especially then."

"Done."

Her lips grow into a wide grin and she leans over and hugs me.

~*~

The next day, my last day with the FBI, Agent Sparks takes me to see my parents at the local county jail, where they're awaiting extradition.

I need closure after all. I need to let go of my past so I can have a future.

It's like the movies. There's a booth with a glass window and a phone that we have to use to talk through.

When I get there, only Mother comes out to see me.

She's not wearing an orange jumpsuit or anything, just a plain black T-shirt and blue jeans. There's no makeup on her face, and her hair is pulled back into a simple ponytail. She looks small and vulnerable, less of an imposing figure than I could ever imagine her being.

I wonder if she's always been this way and I just saw what I wanted. Has my perception changed, or has she?

Maybe both.

When she picks up the handset, I expect her to say something terrible. Really lay into me with the guilt trips and anger, but instead she says in a low voice, "I'm surprised you came."

"I am, too. I wasn't going to."

"Your father couldn't make it." She averts her eyes, her fingers fiddling with the phone cord.

And then we're silent for more than a few seconds, sort of sizing each other up, each passing second increasing in awkwardness.

And then I have to ask. "Why did you keep the birth certificate? Why not get rid of the evidence of Paige's birth when you knew it could be used against you? Why remind me of the safe to begin with? It was intentional, wasn't it?"

She swallows and meets my eyes. "Being in the game isn't easy, as you know. You're always on the run. Always looking behind you. Always making plans and covering tracks. It was exciting when I was younger but . . . it was time for it to be over."

Her words floor me. "You *wanted* to get caught?"

She shrugs. "We were in over our heads. It was too much. Everything had spiraled out of control."

I know the feeling.

"Your father doesn't know." She lowers her voice, as if he might hear her. "He never had anyone who loved him but me, you know."

I don't really understand the comment. Is she making excuses for him?

There are things she's not telling me. About why she was done. Did she do it to protect us? Maybe even a little bit?

I don't know what to say to her, but I don't have to because she keeps talking.

"I know we won't get out of this, no matter how much your father promises me he has it all figured out. Will you come see me sometime? Maybe bring Paige, too?"

"I don't know." How could I? I've spent the last three months running from them and now she wants me to spend time with them willingly? Even just Mother? I guess it helps if they're behind bars. I don't think I can forgive them, but I have to move forward.

I wouldn't be here if Mother hadn't tipped me off about the safe. I bet she even left the car door unlocked on purpose. And all the breaks they kept giving me, when she convinced Father to give me more time . . .

I know eventually I have to make peace with them, even if only in my own mind and heart.

I leave the courthouse a bundle of damaged nerves. All raw sensation and exposed underbelly. Agent Sparks takes me back to the hotel and we order cheeseburgers and raid the mini fridge. I don't know what to think about anything anymore, but I'm glad I talked to my mom. I have to make peace with my past. It's part of who I am.

It's my last night. Tomorrow, they're releasing me back into the wild. Or, you know, back to Castle Cove. I've been avoiding all thoughts of Jared and what's going to happen when I go back, or where I'm going to stay and what I'm going to do. I have to go back, though. Paige is there. Even if I can't have her, even if I can't see her, even if I have to sleep on the street, I'm going to find a way to stay close.

"What am I going to do now?" I ask Agent Sparks.

"Have you ever considered a career in law enforcement?"

CHAPTER TWENTY-FOUR

The next morning, Agent Sparks drops me off at the bus station with a hug and a one-way ticket anywhere.

"If you ever need anything, call me. My card is in there." She nods to the envelope with my ticket. I reach inside and pull out a plain white card with her name, email, and business-phone and cell-phone numbers written in red ink.

"Thank you for everything."

"Good luck in Castle Cove. I don't know if I could live there. Those people are nuts."

"They are." I smile. "But they're my nuts."

I watch her drive away with a sigh and then finger the card in my hand. I wonder what she would do if I called her for a job . . . after I find the money for school and hopefully graduate before I'm thirty-six and too old to be an agent.

I blow out a breath and the business card slips from my fingers and flutters to the pavement.

Bending over, I pick it up. As I stand, my eyes catch on a pair of shoes stopped in front of me.

They're connected to legs encased in dark jeans. A fitted—but not too tight—black T-shirt. At the top is a lovely, recognizable face.

My eyes drink him in. His hair is a mess. His face is scruffy and unshaven. His eyes are watching me as I watch his, our gazes mirroring both hope and caution. He looks delicious. I mean, for god's sake, he's wearing jeans and a T-shirt. But still. Possibly the most attractive thing I've ever seen.

I don't know what to say.

Thankfully, he starts first.

"I have to ask you something."

"Anything."

He pauses for a few seconds. "Were we a lie, too?"

I shake my head. No matter my answer, will it be pointless? Too little too late? How can I tell him the truth and expect him to believe me? "Does it matter how I answer? Would you believe me?"

"It matters."

I bite my lip. I don't deserve his trust, even now that every word is the truth. "I never even told you my real name."

"I know." Then he hesitates and admits, "Actually, I always knew you weren't Ruby."

My heart drops to the concrete floor at my feet. "What?" I can't believe it. "What do you mean, you *always* knew?"

"You might remember when we first met, I wasn't exactly, um . . ." He smiles a little, one corner of his mouth ticking up at the side. "Nice. To you. I knew you were lying about being Ruby. When I first saw you, you were looking for work on the boardwalk. I watched you go into the stores and ask for a job. But then suddenly you were the owner of the new shop and starting a business. It didn't make sense."

I think back to that day at the boardwalk, when he yelled at me for going into the abandoned shop. I didn't realize he had seen so much. He was a distraction to me, even then.

I don't know what to say.

He shrugs and shoves his hands in his pockets before he continues. "I'm a cop. It was easy to look up Ruby and realize it wasn't you. At first, I didn't really know what to think. And it really didn't make sense when you knew things happening around town, and you helped people. You weren't acting like a bad guy. You were kind. I thought maybe you were on the run from something or someone and using Ruby as a cover. I just didn't know what it was. I had hoped you would trust me and talk to me before it came to this."

"Trust is a difficult thing. So hard to gain, so easy to lose. You were right, though. I was on the run. Ruby was a cover, one I never should have used. I should have told you sooner. I should have trusted you." I sigh and look him in the eye. "There's a lot of things I should have done. I'm sorry that I didn't trust you enough to tell you. You did earn my trust, over and over, and I was an idiot."

He smiles a little, just a small upturn of his lips, but it's enough to send my heart racing. "You're not an idiot. I understand why you did what you did. Although, I agree that you should have told me sooner." He moves closer, pulling his hands out of his pockets and I wonder if he's going to touch me, hug me, strangle me, something. But he stops less than a foot away. So close I have to look up at him. "You haven't answered my original question."

I breathe, "We were never a lie. Not to me."

His smile grows. "Good." He glances around the bus depot. "Where are you headed?"

"Oh, you know, LA."

His brows rise. "LA?"

"Yeah, I thought I might audition for a soap opera or something."

His brows furrow. "Really?"

I smack him in the arm with my envelope. "No! I'm going to Castle Cove, obviously. I can't go anywhere else. Not if Paige is still there . . . ?" I hold my breath, waiting for his response. It's something I haven't wanted to think about, Paige's real family coming for her. What if they take her away? What if they don't let me see her? Could I blame them? Would they want someone with such an inauspicious past around their long lost niece or granddaughter or whatever? I wouldn't.

He smiles but tries to suppress it. "She's there. But you . . . is it just Paige you want to go back for?"

She's there. Relief fills me. And my heart flutters with hope at his words. Does he want me to come back for him, too? I can't quite believe it yet.

"Well, you know, I heard the next book club selection is really good."

"Really."

"Not the one they're actually reading, but the one they're pretending to read."

"Of course."

"And I can't miss the next trivia night."

"That would be a shame. You know, I happen to be heading your way. I could give you a ride."

Now I can't hide my smile either. "Yes. Yes, please."

I follow him out of the bus depot and to his car, parked a few rows down in the lot.

We don't speak again until he's driving on the freeway.

"How did you know about the . . . my parents? Because you knew, didn't you. Before the gala."

He nods. "Agent Sparks and her partner clued me in a couple weeks before. The FBI has been on their tail in the past, but they gave the agents the slip a few years ago. The feds picked them back up because of their involvement with Bradford Stone. Your parents were running a con on him. But it didn't work out for them, so he started blackmailing them for a significant amount of money. If they didn't pay him, he planned on taking Paige. He tried to run after you outed them at the gala. The FBI caught him about an hour outside of town and he squealed."

I nod. "I saw him in Portland."

"It sounds like they were using Paige as a backup plan, but they never intended to turn her over to him. Anyway, the FBI was tracking him and your parents. Agent Sparks and the others followed them here. The feds didn't know for sure that you and Paige were even involved. Neither did I, at first, but I started to suspect."

"When?"

"It just made sense. You were related, you were already lying about being Ruby, and they were known cons . . . Then there were the Castle Cove Ninja incidents, and I found you outside their house late at night." He shoots me a look, his brows lifted. "You were in all black. I am a cop, you know."

I flush, chagrined. Of course he knew. "What were you doing by their house?"

"Meeting up with the agents that were tailing them." He smiles at me. "I knew you were planting a tracker on them. I told you about the chief's purchases for a reason. I wasn't sure if you would really steal them, but then . . . I saw the items missing from the archives right after you took them. I didn't know about the jewelry heist but it was fishy when I found the jewels under the pier. I knew you were involved, but I didn't know they were actually your parents or that they were blackmailing you or any of those details."

"Did you hide your tax statements before my birthday party? Which isn't really my birthday, by the way." I bite my lip at the confession, even though he undoubtedly knows.

"I did." He shoots me a quick glance before turning his gaze back to the road. "I knew at that point your parents weren't exactly trustworthy. I couldn't take any chances. I may have also set up a small, separate bank account to see if they would try and take it. Or if you would."

He set it up as a ruse. The man is positively criminal when he wants to be. "I almost used it myself to run again."

"But you didn't."

"No. I didn't. Why didn't you tell me all of this when I came clean and you arrested me?"

"Well, you see, we had a plan to get them before they left with the charity funds, after the gala. But then Ruby's accountant showed up, and you exposed them and came clean. We had to do something to make sure they didn't bail town right away. The only way we could see to keep them here and bring them down was to implicate you. If they thought their plans had worked and you were going to take the fall for their crimes, they would show up to help nail the lid on your coffin. And we would have witnesses, law enforcement, a respected judge . . . and quite a few members of the general public, which wasn't planned but worked out okay even though I wanted to wring Tabby's neck." He shakes his head.

We're quiet for a few minutes while I think over all of the information he's given me, along with everything I've learned over the last few days.

There's a question I'm dying to ask and dreading at the same time.

"What about Paige's real family? Did you contact them?"

"I did. They're coming to Castle Cove in a couple days. They've been making preparations to stay in town for a while."

My heart starts thumping in my chest. Am I going to lose her anyway?

"They seem very anxious to meet her but also concerned about everything she's been through. I explained the whole situation to them. They want to run some DNA tests to be sure, but it's more of a formality. I sent them some pictures and she looks exactly like her parents. They don't want to upset her routine too much, and it sounds like they're open to a sort of joint-custody-type thing, depending on what Paige, I mean, Andrea wants. They're more concerned with her happiness, it seems, than taking her away from everything she has, but they definitely want to be involved. I just thought you should know. They seem like good people."

I nod, not able to speak, my throat swelling with emotion.

When we reach Castle Cove, I expect him to go to his house, but instead he heads down Main Street and pulls in front of Ruby's.

"What are we doing here?"

"You'll see."

I follow him up the familiar sidewalk, past the sign with the whimsical font that reads *Ruby's Readings and Cosmic Shop*, and into the store.

Unlike the first time I walked in, it's not an empty, dusty space.

It's full of people and chatter.

In one corner, Ruby is laughing at Mrs. Olsen, who's holding up a very phallic lighthouse glass sculpture with an arrested expression on her face.

A few more ladies from book club are filling up the space, plus Mrs. Hale and the Newsomes. Ben and Tabby are arguing by the door that leads to the living space, Troy is trying to tickle Eleanor with a peacock feather . . . it's all so wonderfully familiar.

"You're here!" an even more familiar voice calls out, and then footsteps are thudding across the wood floor in my direction.

"Paige!"

She throws her arms around me and the room erupts in cheers.

I flush, embarrassed to be on display at such an emotional moment. Even more people are hovering in the doorway to the reading room.

I make myself step back, but I can't let go of Paige yet, my hands clenched on her shoulders. "You're wearing new clothes."

"Tabby made me go shopping with her while we were waiting for you to come home. She said it was the only thing that would make her not want to lie around and eat her feelings." She rolls her eyes, but her smile is wide and bright.

I can't believe I'm here. And she's here. And everything will be okay. Everything will really be okay.

Then Tabby is jumping in between us to give me hugs and I'm lost in the shuffle of people all wanting to talk to me, like I didn't just see all of them a few days ago.

Finally, I get a chance to ask. "Why are you all here?"

Ruby answers. "It's a welcome-home party." She's smiling, her blond hair braided around the crown of her head with little white flowers stuck in the creases.

At my confusion, she explains. "Not this building, home, but Castle Cove, home." Then she laughs a little and pats Jared on the arm. "This is your real home."

I'm not sure if she means Jared or Castle Cove. Maybe both.

But the truth is I don't even know where I'm sleeping tonight. Jared hasn't said anything explicit, and while we've danced around the issue, I'm not a hundred percent sure he even wants to be with me still. There's no way we can just pick up where we left off, right?

I can't ask him now anyway because I'm being herded through the house and out to the backyard. There's a barbeque set up. Mr. Bingel is wearing an apron and flipping burgers. Children run around in the sprinklers and grown-ups sit around talking and eating and laughing.

I spend an hour or more answering questions and talking while we eat and sit in the warm summer sunshine.

Paige stays near me almost the whole time. I meet Jared's eyes a few times across the backyard but it's not until people start leaving that he comes my way.

I've spent the last half hour talking to Ruby about her time in India. When Jared stops in our little circle, she finishes her story and then Mrs. Ramsey comes over to ask her a question. They walk away and then it's just Jared and I standing in the corner of the yard.

The first time we've been alone since we got here.

"So can I—?"

"Are you—?"

We both stop and laugh awkwardly.

"You go first," I say, wanting to stall before I have to humble myself yet again and beg for a place to stay.

"I was just wondering if you were about ready to go."

"Where are we going?"

He shoves his hands in his pockets and squints at me. "Home. I was hoping. My home, I mean. That is, unless you—"

"No." I stop him. "There is no 'unless' for me."

"What were you going to say, before?"

"Actually, I wasn't sure you would want me to stay with you so I was . . ." I flail a little. "Preparing myself to ask."

His eyes flare for a moment and then he smiles, a slow upward slide of his lips. After a quick glance around, he grabs my hand and tugs me around the side of the house.

"Where are we—"

My words are interrupted with a searing kiss and all thoughts flee. He leans against the wall and pulls me against him, his hands sliding down my body until I groan into his mouth.

It would be so easy to just lose myself in this right now, but I need to know.

"Jared." I pull away.

"Yeah." His voice is throaty and his eyes are hooded.

"What does this mean?"

"What does what mean?" He nuzzles my neck.

"I mean . . . you still want me?"

"Nothing's changed, Charlotte."

He said my name. My name, on his lips. *Finally*.

My breath catches in my throat, and I can't speak. He must misinterpret my silence as confusion, because he keeps speaking.

"I love you. Of course I still want to be with you. I want you and Paige to live with me—whenever we can keep her—and we'll figure the rest out." He pauses, his eyes searching mine in the fading light. "That's what you want, too, right?"

"It is. I love you, too."

And then we're kissing again and I have to force myself to push him away so I can meet his eyes. "But I'm getting a job. You're not going to trust fund me into submission."

"Okay." He bends over and kisses my neck. "As long as you don't rob the neighbors or run around the streets at night in your ninja outfit. Although wearing it in the bedroom is up for negotiation."

I laugh and shove him in the shoulder. "And I'm going to school. Or something. I'm going to take classes."

"What kind of classes?" He's still nuzzling my neck and the words brush against my skin, making me shiver.

"How about criminal justice?"

He chuckles, resting his forehead against mine. "That would be extraordinary."

The End

About the Author

Mary Frame is a full-time mother and wife with a full-time job. She has no idea how she manages to write novels except that it involves copious amounts of wine. She doesn't enjoy writing about herself in the third person, but she does enjoy reading, writing, dancing, and damaging the eardrums of her coworkers when she randomly decides to sing to them.

She lives in Reno, Nevada, with her husband, two children, and a border collie named Stella.

She LOVES hearing from readers and will not only respond but likely begin stalking them while tossing out hearts and flowers and rainbows! If that doesn't creep you out, email her at maryframeauthor at gmail.com.

To sign up for Mary's newsletter, find other books she's written, or see what she's working on, visit her website at www.authormaryframe.com.

Follow her on Twitter: marewulf

Like her Facebook author page: www.facebook.com/AuthorMaryFrame

CPSIA information can be obtained
at www.ICGtesting.com
Printed in the USA
LVHW090513241218
601580LV00001B/78/P

9 781983 610608